Missing
in the
Mountains

by T. S. FIELDS

rising moon

*The publisher gives special thanks to
Ronda Booty's seventh-grade class (1998–1999) at
Aspen Middle School in Aspen, Colorado,
and Julia Wilson's fourth-grade class (1998–1999)
at Marshall Elementary School in Flagstaff, Arizona,
for their insightful commentary.*

Composed and manufactured in the United States of America.

The use of trade names does not imply an endorsement
by the product manufacturer.

FIRST IMPRESSION 1999
ISBN 0-87358-741-3 (sc)

02 03 04   4 3 2

Fields, Terri, 1948–
Missing in the mountains / by T.S. Fields
p. cm.
Summary: To avoid further encounters with a bully on the ski slope,
Jarod and his younger sister cross over the ski area boundary, become
stranded in a snow cave, and fearfully wait to be rescued.
[1. Skis and skiing—Fiction. 2. Brothers and sisters—Fiction. 3.
Survival—Fiction. 4. Bullies—Fiction.] I. Title.
PZ7.F47918 Mi 1999
[Fic]—dc21   99-040048

To many memorable family adventures.
(W. T. F .F. Y. W. A)

And to Jan Fields, Suzie, and John Scher
who've been patiently waiting.

A large thank you to the following people whose advice
and expertise were indispensable in creating this book:
Val Paleski, Search and Rescue Coordinator, Coconino
County Sheriff's Office; B.J. Boyle, Arizona Snowbowl Ski
Patrol; Tom Caretto, snowboarder; Jeff Fields and Lori Fields,
Barbara Bernstein, and Aimee Jackson for editing advice.
A very special thank you to teacher Patricia Jo Carpenter
and her fifth grade class (1998–1999) at Desert Vista
Elementary School in Apache Junction, Arizona.

CHAPTER 1

"**S**mile, I want to take one more picture of the two of you." Jarod and Jennifer Golden's mother pointed a camera at her children. "You both look so cute together!"

Jarod groaned. "Oh, great," he muttered under his breath. "That's just what I've always wanted to look—cute, in a picture with my little sister. Yuck!"

"Come on, Jarod, smile!" Mrs. Golden said. Jarod shook his head, took out his beige knit hat, and pulled it over his eyes.

"Jarod, take off that hat!" his mother demanded. "How will anyone ever know it's you?"

"That's the plan," Jarod mumbled as he reluctantly pushed the hat out of his eyes. Jarod was almost twelve, and he could snowboard the steepest slopes with the best of them. But not today. Today, he was about to ride the baby chairlift up to the beginner slope with his little sister. Even more embarrassing, his mother was pointing a camera at them so she'd have recorded memories of the event.

Just then, Jarod heard a taunting voice. "Oh, boy! I wish *my* mommy could come take pictures of me, too!" Jarod thought there was something familiar about the deep, mocking sound of that voice. He glanced over, but he could see only the back of a big guy in a dark brown parka. He probably didn't know the guy anyway. In fact, Jarod decided that if he was lucky, he wouldn't run into a single person he knew during his family's ski vacation.

The lift line continued to move forward, and Jarod and Jennifer were finally at the front. As the chair swept under them, Mrs. Golden waved and called, "You two have fun!"

I doubt that, Jarod thought.

"This is so great!" Jennifer said as the lift took them up the tiny hill. "It's the first time we've been back in the snow since we moved from Colorado. I'm so glad that my asthma is finally better and I can ski again."

Jarod noticed that Jennifer barely paused for breath before she began again. "See, I used to wish I was you because you got to go snowboarding every week and I had to stay home because of my bad breathing. But I'm okay now." She giggled. "And it's *so* fun to be here!" She paused and looked at Jarod. "Aren't you going to say anything?"

"How can I get a word in edgewise," Jarod said. "We're almost at the top. Get ready to get off."

Jennifer pointed the tips of her skis up, and Jarod raised his board slightly as the lift deposited them onto the snow at the top of the mountain. Two girls near them were giggling as they started down the mountain. "This is so exciting," one said. "Yeah, but it's scary, too!" the other replied. "Hey, here I go!" shouted the first, barely moving.

Jarod's eyes followed the girl as she started down the hill in a wide snowplow. He shook his head. No one on this hill had a clue about what to do. He sighed and wondered how people could even think this was skiing. "Jen, you go ahead," he said, trying to play the part of good brother. "I'll watch and then catch up to you."

Jennifer beamed. "Okay. I think I'll remember how to be good. That's what Mom says."

"Mom doesn't know how to ski at all," Jarod replied. That's why he was stuck here. His mother was too worried about Jennifer's breathing, especially at this high altitude, to let her go off by herself. Jarod had been recruited to ski with her.

Jennifer pushed off and began making her way slowly down the slope. Jarod had to admit that her form wasn't bad, even if she did look a little like a Pepto Bismo bottle in her bright pink ski outfit. In fact, Jarod decided, she wasn't even such a bad sister. But he wanted to be out with his friends, challenging them to the steepest hills and the best rides. Instead, his friends were all snowboarding the exciting slopes together, and he was on the bunny hill with his eight-year-old sister. Jarod sighed, saw that Jennifer was about halfway down the slope, and pushed off himself.

Jarod tried to do a little carving, even though the slope was barely steep enough to make it worthwhile. About halfway down, he forced himself to stop and check on Jennifer, whom he had already passed. Cupping his hands around his eyes to cut the sun's glare, he looked up and saw that she was still carefully skiing above him.

Jarod looked around. Just a little bit closer to the top was the guy in the dark brown jacket. Jarod watched as the guy put his skis together, started to lose his balance, and then crouched so hard into a snowplow that he was almost in the splits. The guy was big and pretty funny to watch, Jarod decided.

Just then, the guy cut right in front of a little boy, and the boy started to cry. You bully! Jarod thought. Too bad someone doesn't ski in front of you!

Jarod watched as the guy ramrodded his way through several other little kids. He half-shoved a little boy in bibs, and the boy tumbled over. The jerk never even looked back or said he was sorry. The few adults on the hill were too focused on their own shaky skiing to notice. Somebody ought to stop that guy! Jarod thought. But no one did. Bullies always seemed to get away with doing awful things. Jarod watched a minute more. That bully almost looked like someone he knew, but who? he wondered. As the guy got closer, Jarod's mouth fell open. "Eric Lehman!" he gasped.

When Jarod lived in Colorado, every kid at Steck Elementary had known to stay away from Eric. He had been as tall as his teacher by fourth grade. Some kids said that Eric had been held back in school twice, but *no one* ever said that to his face. In fact, no one said anything to Eric. Jarod remembered all the lunches Eric had taken from the third graders in Jarod's class. Jarod missed a lot of things about Colorado, but Eric definitely wasn't one of them.

Jarod cringed as Eric pushed a little girl into the snow and shouted, "Out of my way!" He sure hadn't changed much, Jarod thought. He watched Eric snowplow and wondered how such a huge guy could be so uncoordinated on skis. Then suddenly, Jarod had an idea. Grinning, he said quietly, "Hey, Eric, this is going to be for every kid you ever were mean to!"

Jarod watched carefully. He knew his timing had to be perfect. Then, just as Eric got right above him, Jarod pulled one of his best flatland tricks—a terrific tail slide. Snow flew, and Eric

4

was covered in white.

Jarod laughed to himself. The bully didn't look so tough any more. Feeling good, Jarod didn't stay around to watch Eric brush himself off. Instead, he tried a few more tricks and felt the thrill of a perfect switch stance.

Then suddenly Jarod remembered he was supposed to be watching out for his sister. He'd almost forgotten her! He came to an abrupt halt and stared up the slope, then quickly realized he didn't have to worry. Jennifer was fine. Dressed in her fluorescent pink ski outfit, she was hard to miss. But If she kept going this slowly, they would never get any runs in. They'd already missed more than half a day on the slopes because his mother hadn't wanted Jennifer to get too tired. He couldn't believe that their mom made them wait at the hotel all morning and then get only a half-day lift ticket. He'd tried to explain that the snow was much better before everyone had been on it all morning, but his mother hadn't listened. She'd only talked about the altitude and not tiring Jennifer out too much.

"Come on, Jen," he called. "Hurry up." He'd barely gotten the words out when he felt something grab his throat. Then Jarod started to gasp for breath. "Let go!" he tried to say, but the pressure on his throat got worse. From the corner of his eye, he could see a hand coming out of a brown parka, and a sinking feeling told him who it belonged to and why it was squeezing his throat.

Jarod could hear Eric laughing. "Not such hot stuff now, are you? You know, when I let go of your throat, if you don't pass out first, I'm going to shove your ugly face into the snow. Let's see how hot you are to mess with me then."

Jarod could feel Eric's hand squeezing harder around his throat. "Help!" he tried to call. On this whole crowded ski slope, someone had to be noticing that he was getting choked to death! "Help!" he tried to wave, but no one stopped! He could feel himself starting to black out, and then just as he thought he couldn't stand it any more, Eric let go. Jarod began to gasp. As he rubbed his throat with his hand, he wondered what had made Eric finally loosen his grip. And then he looked down.

Jennifer was sitting on the ground. "I saw that guy hurting you! I was scared, but then I thought if I just ran into him, he'd have to let go of you, and it worked! I pushed as hard as I could right by his knees, and his skis took off with him on them. I don't think he could stop once he started—well, that is, at least until he fell." She pointed down the slope. "I think that's him on the ground way down there." Jennifer looked up at Jarod. "You okay?"

"I'm fine." Jarod sighed. It was embarrassing to have his little sister coming to his rescue. He tried to change the subject. "Give me one of your poles, and I'll pull you up."

Jennifer smiled, "I saved you, huh? See, I'm not so bad to have around. What'd you do to make him choke you anyway? Aren't you going to say thanks or anything?"

"Thanks or anything," Jarod said with a grin as he pulled Jennifer to her feet.

"Why'd he choke you?"

"The guy's just a jerk, okay? Now let's get going!" He rubbed his neck again.

Jennifer didn't move. "I just want to know why he was

choking you."

"And then you'll start moving?" Jarod asked.

"Uh-huh."

"All right," Jarod said. "It was like this. I watched him push through all those beginner kids up near the top, so when he got near me, I did a flatland trick that sort of accidentally on purpose got a little snow in his face. Okay. Now you know, so let's go."

"I don't like bullies. They're mean for no reason," Jennifer said. "You were brave to stand up to him!"

Jarod felt himself blush. "It was no big deal. Let's go."

Jennifer pushed off. She had barely gone a foot when she stopped. Jarod boarded over to her. "Now what?" he asked.

Jennifer's worried eyes stared up at her older brother. "Well, I think that's that mean guy with the bad temper down there looking up at us, and he looks real mad, don't you think?"

CHAPTER 2

"**I** think he's waiting for us to come down." Jennifer glanced up at her brother. "What're we going to do?"

"We're...well...we're...we're not even sure it's Eric," Jarod said. He needed time to think.

"Eric?" Jennifer asked. "How do you know his name?"

"Uh...I think he might be this guy who used to go to Steck."

"Steck!" Jennifer said in surprise. Then her eyes opened wide. "Wait! I remember. Eric was that bully guy in the sixth grade when I was in kindergarten, right? Wow! We all heard about him. On the playground people would say, 'Watch out. Eric Lehman's going to get you!' and everyone would run away screaming. Jarod, what are we going to do? I...I shoved him, and I made him fall down. I don't even want to think what he'll do to me."

Jennifer plunked herself down in the snow. "Let's just wait here for a while. As long as we don't ski down the slope, I don't think he's going to climb back up it."

Jarod pulled his hat off and stuffed it in his backpack. He wondered how this day could just keep getting worse. He hadn't wanted to ski with Jen in the first place. He hadn't wanted to go on the bunny hill, and now he certainly did not want to stay on this little slope the whole day.

"Jen, stop panicking! Even if it is Eric, he is already at the bottom. He's not going to do anything to us with all those people around."

"Oh yeah?" Jennifer said. "Weren't there lots of people around when he was choking you?"

"That was different," Jarod said. "The people around were all beginner skiers, and they were so busy trying to concentrate on not falling down that they probably never even noticed me. But it's different at the bottom. People are standing around, watching what's going on. Really."

Jennifer still didn't budge. Jarod sighed, "Okay, tell you what. You just stay here. I'll go down first and prove that we're going to be fine."

"Wait." Jennifer struggled to get up. "I don't think you should go. Jarod, he's going to—"

Jarod cut her off. "I'm leaving. You coming or not?"

"Wait! I'm coming," Jennifer said, and then more softly, she added, "but I don't think I should."

"I told you it's going to be fine." Jarod pushed off and started down the slope again. In spite of his brave words, Jarod felt his knees wobble and his heart pound. As he got closer to the bottom, he could almost feel Eric staring up at him and following his pathway down the slope.

"Okay," Jarod told himself, "I know that nothing is going to happen at the bottom. What I told Jen about him leaving us alone is right...but we sure don't have to run right into the guy." He veered off to the left, stopping long enough to call over his shoulder, "Jen, follow me. Don't go straight down."

Jarod boarded down the far left side of the slope and

quickly reached the bottom. It seemed to him that it was taking Jennifer hours to reach him. *Come on!* he called silently. *Hurry up!* He looked up the mountain at his sister and then over his shoulder to see if Eric was getting any closer. Unfortunately, it seemed to him that the jerk was getting closer faster than his sister. *Come on, hurry!* he silently pleaded to Jennifer.

When she reached the bottom, Jarod called, "Don't stop. Just start skating over to that other tow." He pointed. Jennifer bobbed her head okay and kept going. Jarod caught up with her quickly. "Hurry. Move faster. He's following us."

"Where're we going?" Jennifer asked.

"Where he can't go," Jarod replied. "Just come on. I'll explain later."

Jennifer struggled to keep up with Jarod. She was panting hard by the time Jarod finally stopped in another tow line. Fortunately, there weren't very many people in front of them, and Jarod felt his body hit the seat of the chair at the same time he heard Eric's voice call out, "Hey, mommy's little poster boy! I'm not finished with you!"

As the chairlift began to carry them up the hill, Jarod turned to face the bully, and extending his arm in the air, he raised his fist to Eric.

"Jarod!" Jennifer exclaimed. "I'm not sure you should have done that!"

The chairlift pulled them higher until the brown jacket was just a small speck beneath them. "Maybe, but Eric can't reach us now!"

Jennifer swung her legs a little and the chair rocked. "It

was dumb, if you ask me."

"I didn't ask you."

Jennifer shrugged, "Yeah, but it's both of us that are going to get beaten up if he finds us."

Jarod shifted the backpack he was carrying. "He's not going to find us!"

"Yeah? I hope you're right," Jennifer said. "But how do you know?"

Jarod grinned. "Simple. This chair takes us up to the intermediate and advanced slopes. And as for that jerk, he's not good enough to follow us up here. The way he skis, he'd break his neck up on these slopes. And he knows it. So we're done with him! And I'm glad I told him off. We're going to have a great day on the mountain, and he's going back to the bunny hill." Jarod rubbed his gloves together. "Good thinking to come over here. You can thank your big brother, huh?"

Jennifer's eyes grew large. "Maybe it wasn't such a good idea. I don't think I'm good enough to get down any of those hard slopes."

"You'll be okay skiing intermediate slopes. Your form is good. All you need is confidence," Jarod said as he glanced down the slope.

Jennifer's face clouded over, "I really can't..."
But before she could say more, Jarod interrupted. "You can do this. I mean it. I watched you the whole way down the bunny hill. You were doing fine."

"You're not just saying that?"

Jarod shook his head no.

"Then you really think I'm a good skier?" Jennifer smiled.

11

"Yeah, I do."

"Okay, then," Jennifer said, "If you think I can do the intermediate slopes, I guess I can. At least, I hope I can."

The chair slowed enough for them to hop off. Jarod could feel the sense of excitement that ran through his body each time he stood on top of a snow-covered mountain. Ski runs stretched out in every direction as far as he could see, and Jarod felt as if he could practically fly if he could get on a really good slope. Grinning at the thought of catching some air, he heard Jennifer call, "Hey, there's a sign over there that tells which runs are which. Let's see which slope we want to ski. I wonder which one is easiest."

Jennifer carefully skied over to a big wooden sign with pictures of white slopes and green trees. On each white hill was a colored line and a name. Jennifer stood reading every one of them.

"Jen!" Jarod called. "Let's not stand here and read all day. How about if we just try Rough Rider?"

Jennifer shook her head. "No way! Even the name sounds hard, and the black line means it's advanced. I can't do that." She pointed to another slope with a blue line running down it. "How about this one? It's intermediate, and besides, I like the name—Sunday Stroll. Let's try it."

Jarod continued to gaze longingly at Rough Rider.

Jennifer turned to start down Sunday Stroll, and then she realized that Jarod was not behind her. She turned to call him, and what she saw made her gasp. "Jarod," she screamed. "Take off! Go! Hurry! Eric's right behind us!"

CHAPTER 3

Jennifer didn't have to say it twice. Jarod whipped around to see the bully heading directly toward them. It was impossible, but Eric looked as if he'd gotten even bigger, and he sure looked mad. Jarod jumped into action. "Jen. Start skiing now!" He ordered, "And don't be so slow! Move it!"

"And don't be so slow," came a mocking voice behind him. "Golden, it isn't going to matter what you and your sister do now. You should have kept your mouth shut and stayed away from me. But you didn't. Now you're going to pay."

"Go, Jennifer!" Jarod called again. He was amazed to see his sister take off at a halfway decent speed. Jarod tried to stay right with her so that he could at least try to protect her when Eric caught up with them. "Stupid, stupid me!" he told himself. "I had to try to be a big man, and now look at this mess."

The bully yelled from behind them. "Look at the two little scared bunny rabbits try to hop, hop away. Well, you won't get very far!"

Jarod heard Jennifer gulp. "Don't cry, Jen. Just ski! Concentrate on skiing!" He kept his board near Jennifer. His heart was pounding in his throat. Jarod had no doubt that if Eric got hold of him, he'd end up going down the slope in a ski patrol toboggan.

All of a sudden, Jennifer's skis hit an icy patch and Jarod

heard her scream. He could see one of her legs start to slide away from her, but somehow, she was able to right herself before she fell. "I feel out of control! Can we try to stop?" she called to Jarod.

"You might as well," came a deep voice from close behind them.

"Hurry, Jen!" Jarod called.

"I'm trying, Jarod! He wasn't supposed to be here. He's going to catch us. I know it!"

And then a voice coming from right behind them called, "Get ready to get bashed into snowmen."

Jennifer's knees started to shake, and then they buckled underneath her.

Jarod skidded to a stop when he saw his sister fall. "Jen, get up and ski! Now!" he shouted.

"I can't," she cried. "I'm too scared to move."

Jarod glanced up to see Eric getting closer. If he just carved hard, Jarod knew that Eric could never catch him. He could take off this second and be safe. He looked at his sister, whose large brown eyes made her look like a frightened deer. Jarod took a deep breath. He wasn't leaving.

Jarod quickly unfastened his board and held it like a weapon as Eric got closer. He tried not to shake as the bully was almost upon them. And just then, he saw Eric's left ski hit the small patch of ice that had almost tripped Jennifer. Eric skidded on the ice and fell down hard. Half-sitting, half-lying on the backs of his skis, he began to slide quickly down the hill. He let out a loud yell as he slipped down the mountain. Jarod and Jennifer watched in open-mouthed amazement until

Eric was finally able to turn his body to the side and stop his fall.

"Wow." Jennifer sighed. "That was too scary. I really thought he was going to get us, didn't you?"

Jarod didn't answer. Eric had gotten up from his fall. Now he was looking up the hill and staring at them with his hands on his hips.

Jennifer shook her head, and her blond hair swung gently. "If he was mad before, now he's going to be... Oh, my gosh! He's taking off his skis and just standing there waiting for us to have to pass him."

Jarod felt a little sick. He knew that the only reason they had escaped Eric was because the guy was such a poor skier. In fact, the only advantage they had was to keep him on his skis. Standing on firm footing in the snow, Eric was really scary. To make everything worse, Jarod noticed, Eric was standing exactly where the slope narrowed. It wouldn't be easy to get around him.

Jarod took a deep breath. "Okay, Jen, here's what we're going to have to do. If we don't get past him really fast, he's going to grab us. So forget that you're scared. When you get to his spot, you've got to zoom by so that he can't grab you. I'm going to try to ride by him at the same time to distract him, but I don't know if we can both hit that narrow spot together."

"I don't want to try," Jennifer said on the verge of tears.

Down below them, the two could see Eric pounding the fist of one hand into the palm of his other hand. Jarod commanded, "You've got to get past him. Don't even look at him! Just ski as fast as you can."

They took off together, but as they got closer, Jarod had a really bad feeling about what was going to happen. "Jen," Jarod called. "Wait. Stop there! Don't go down any farther."

CHAPTER 4

Jennifer shifted her weight and tried to stop. Coming to a halt next to her, Jarod said, "I changed my mind. There's no way we're both going to get past him. It's too narrow there."

Jennifer leaned on her ski poles and then reached around to release her bindings.

"What're you doing?" Jarod asked.

"If we're going to stay here for a while, I just thought I'd take my skis off and sit down."

"This is crazy!" Jarod said. "He's sitting down there. You're sitting up here. We're on a ski slope, not a sitting slope." His hazel eyes flashed first at the bully and then at his sister. "Who'd ever believe this whole thing!"

Jennifer scooped up a snowball. "I believe it." She looked very solemn. "I guess I'll sit here all day if I have to. It's better than running into that bully!"

"That's not the answer!" Jarod replied.

Jennifer bit her lip. "Well, okay, then what is the answer?"

"I don't know!"

Jarod looked around. There just had to be a way out of this. He looked up the hill. It would be a hard climb to get all the way back to the top, especially with Jennifer's short legs. But if they didn't want to go up, and they couldn't go down, and they didn't want to spend the rest of the day in the same spot, what was left? Jarod looked around, stumped. Stupid Eric was probably enjoying the fact that he was completely ruining their day, but Jarod didn't see an alternative to staying where they were. As if things couldn't get worse, Jarod noticed that the sun had disappeared and snowflakes had begun silently drifting downward.

His eyes searched around the slope again. At the far side of the the slope there was only bright orange netting with an out-of-bounds sign attached to it.

Jarod had seen these signs hundreds of times when he was riding, but he'd never given them much thought before. He stared over at the sign, remembering a conversation he'd had with a couple of snowboarders at the ski lodge. When he'd asked them what slopes they liked at this resort, they'd laughed and said the ones they'd made themselves. Jarod stared at the netting and warning sign. Maybe there was a way out of this after all!

"Jen, stay right there. I just want to check something." Jarod traversed over to the sign that read "Ski Area Boundary—Danger! Do Not Cross." He leaned over the netting. It was hard to see for sure through the patch of pine trees, but he didn't think the snow looked any different there. In fact, it looked exactly the way it did on the slope, except there were no skiers' ruts and—even better, Jarod thought—there was no bully waiting there.

Jarod rode back over to Jennifer and told her his plan. "You want to do what?" Her voice rose in shocked amazement. "Haven't we got enough trouble?"

"It'll be okay," Jarod said. "Some guys in the ski lodge told me all about it. They said that the ski patrol just puts up those signs to keep the best snow for themselves. They said they go out of bounds every day and it's great."

"Isn't that against all the rules?"

"It's probably against the rules for bullies to ruin skiers' days, too, but that isn't stopping Eric. Think about it, Jen. He'll never be able to find us if we get through those trees. We'll be off making our own slope. He'll have no idea where we are."

Jennifer piled a snowball on top of the ones she'd already made. "I just don't know. What if it gets real hard in the out-of-bounds part? Then what?"

Jarod sighed. "Jen, why would it be any harder on one side of the netting than the other? I couldn't see much because of the trees, but what I did see looked just like this exactly."

Jennifer didn't say anything. She just put another snowball on top of all the others. At the rate she was going, she would soon have a little fort. She forced herself to look down the slope at the bully, only he wasn't so far down the slope any more. He was climbing back up to them! "I'm not done with you," he called, his voice getting louder.

"We could throw these at him," Jennifer said, pointing to the snowballs she had made.

"Like that would really stop him!" Jarod said. "Come on, Jen, please, before it's too late!"

"Okay, okay." She stood up and followed Jarod over to the side of the slope. He held up the net for Jennifer and turned to look down at the bully. He was just about to call, "So long, sucker," when Jennifer warned, "Don't you dare say one more thing to that bully. You'll make him so mad that he'll come find us wherever we are!"

Then taking a deep breath, Jennifer ducked under the net and, so softly that Jarod couldn't hear, she whispered, "Please keep us safe." Then two figures, one in bright pink and one in muted tans and greens, moved beyond the warning sign.

Moments later, they had traversed through a line of pine trees and onto a silent, vast world of untouched powder. Jarod grinned. "Wow! This is the most amazing snow I've ever seen."

"Yeah, and the slope doesn't even look that steep!" Jennifer said with excitement.

At first, Jennifer tried to keep the groomed slope in her vision, but as she skied on, she realized that Jarod had been right. This really was no harder than where they had been, and it was fun not to have to dodge all the other skiers or worry about Eric. Finally, she stopped watching to see how to get back on the groomed slope. She just followed Jarod as he blazed ahead. It felt as if they truly were in their own world. Jennifer skied her careful but parallel form, and Jarod cut out with one trick after another.

The snowflakes had gotten a little larger and were coming a little faster now. It was almost as if even the snow knew how exciting all of this was. Jarod let out a war whoop. Jennifer whooped back, but their loud voices were somehow softened by the quiet, unexplored area around them.

Finally, Jarod stopped and let Jennifer catch up with him. She was smiling. "You were right, Jarod. I'm glad we went under the net. It beats sitting there waiting for that bully, and the snow is so nice here. There aren't even any icy patches." Then she stopped and a momentary look of fear came into her eyes. "You do know how we get down to the bottom, don't you?"

Jarod picked up some snow and squashed it against Jen's black velvet hat. "Well, not exactly, but think about it. There's only one way to go, and that's down. So when we get to the bottom of the hill, we'll see the lodge or the road. Either way, we can't get lost, so let's just have fun!"

With that, he took off, made a 360-degree turn, and kept going. He found some little ledges and made a few spectacular jumps. It all felt so good that he laughed out loud. Whatever Jeff, Rick, and David were doing today, it wasn't as good as the run he was getting right here, right now. Jarod thought about how much he begged to have been allowed to ski with his friends rather than Jen, but here he was and now it wasn't even all that bad.

Realizing he'd been moving pretty fast, Jarod stopped and waited for Jennifer to catch up with him. Up above he could see her sure, steady form making its way down toward him. As he waited, he looked around. It seemed to him that they had been being pulled to the left. But it was hard to tell because there were no real markers. Besides, what he had told Jennifer was true. They couldn't get lost. They weren't going to go uphill, and when they got to the bottom, they'd find the lodge. The snow was coming even harder now, and Jarod took the goggles from his jacket pocket and pulled them over his eyes.

When Jennifer reached him, he could see she was huffing like she was out of breath. "I think I need a spray," she gasped. From her pocket, she pulled a small white and silver inhaler, put it in her mouth, and breathed in deeply.

Jarod looked at Jennifer carefully and tried not to be scared. He listened. She wasn't making that awful wheezing sound. That was a good sign. Sometimes, the inhaler was all she needed when the asthma started, and sometimes...his parents had to rush her to the hospital where doctors hooked her up to some kind of IV. What would he do if this was one of those times the inhaler just didn't work? Who was going to help them up here?

CHAPTER 5

Jennifer took a second puff of her inhaler, and Jarod waited, not quite knowing what else to do. Then Jennifer capped the inhaler and stuck it back in her pocket. "That's much better," she said.

"You sure?" Jarod asked.

"Of course I'm sure. I know when I can breathe and when I can't. I'm fine."

Jarod didn't want to take any chances. How many times had he heard his mother worry that Jennifer's asthma could get so bad that she could die. She seemed to be okay, but he said, "Maybe we'd better rest a little bit here. I mean, what would we do if, you know, the inhaler didn't work?"

Jennifer sighed. "Look who's the one trying to be the safe child now!" She stuck her tongue out at Jarod. "But I suppose you're right." She plunked herself down in the snow.

Jarod sat down, too, but only for a minute. Then he got an idea. "See that area over there," he said and pointed.

Jennifer squinted through her goggles and looked in that direction, but it was hard to see much except falling whiteness.

"I think it might be steeper over there." Jarod squinted harder and continued. "I can't tell for sure, but it seems like it might be a good place for some great tricks. Why don't you rest for a few more minutes and come straight down where we are now. I'll head off over there, see if I can hit some jibs, and then I'll ride back to where you are."

Jennifer squinted again through her goggles. "It's snowing so hard. I don't know how you can tell how steep it is over there, but go ahead. I don't want the steep part. This is fine for me. I'll rest for a couple more minutes and meet you."

Jarod stood. "Watch this!" he said and headed off further to the left. Because the snow was coming down so fast in such big flakes, he didn't see a mogul until his board hit it, and he almost lost his balance, but then the slope evened out. Feeling a tremendous rush of wind and snow, he carved fast and hard. Suddenly, he heard a strange sound that seemed loud in all the silence. While he was still trying to figure out what it was, he found himself losing his balance, and the ground under him seemed to give way.

Jarod reached out as he felt himself fall, but there was nothing to catch hold of. He felt his board come loose from his feet, and his body turned and twisted as if it had been caught in a washing machine. He couldn't stop his body from spinning, and he couldn't understand what was happening to him.

With snow pushing at him from every direction, Jarod felt as if he had been forever trapped in turning whiteness. Finally, he felt himself stop swirling. He gasped for air. He wanted to push away the snow that clung to his eyebrows and nose, but he couldn't move. He felt himself shiver. He tried to look around, but everything seemed so hazy. There was a noise in the distance, but he couldn't tell what it was. He tried to make his hand move toward his face, but his hand seemed to be locked away somewhere.

Jarod forced himself to open his eyes. He shook his pounding head. In the far distance, he thought he heard someone screaming words he could almost understand. He tried to concentrate. "Don't be dead, Jarod. Please don't be dead," the voice screamed. But the snow was falling so fast, and he was so cold. Since he couldn't move, he tried to close his eyes and ignore the screams.

From up above, Jennifer had tried to watch her brother as he threaded his way through the steep slope, glad she hadn't followed him. It looked like very tough maneuvering. But Jarod didn't seem to mind. Jennifer couldn't really see him that well through the falling snow, especially since he was wearing muted colors, but she heard him whoop a couple of times, so she figured he must be having fun.

Finally, feeling rested and breathing easily, Jennifer stood up and grabbed her poles. Just as she was getting ready to push off, she heard a strange rumbling noise, and then to her surprise, there was a huge wall of snow that seemed to break off near Jarod and grow larger as it got closer to him. She screamed, "Jarod, get out of the way! Watch out!" She wasn't sure he heard, and even if he had, she wasn't sure there was any way for him to move away from the giant block of careening snow, but she screamed anyway because it was all she could think of to do.

In the next minute, the snow had covered Jarod, and he was tumbling inside the white mass. An avalanche! Jennifer thought. How could they be where there was an avalanche?

Jennifer strained to see her brother in the white mass. What if he were buried in all that snow? How could he breathe? How long did he have for her to get to him and help?

Jennifer pushed off with her poles. "I'm coming!" she called, hoping somehow Jarod could hear her. "Hold on, I'm coming to help!" she yelled again, but there was no movement from below and no answer.

She had only skied a few feet when her uphill ski caught an edge, and she quickly found herself sitting on the ground again. "No!" She uttered the single word in great frustration. How could she possibly help Jarod if she was going to fall down every thirty seconds. What if Jarod couldn't get any air? Why couldn't she be a better skier! She felt shivery. She tried to move faster and fell again. This was getting her nowhere.

"Jarod," she screamed, hoping for an answer. But there was only silence, and the absolute quiet was scarier than the loudest roar. She could feel her eyes fill with tears. She forced herself to get up again and ski very cautiously over toward the spot where Jarod had pointed. Just as she was at the last place she had seen him, she fell again. "Oh, no," she yelped, covering her head with her hands and waiting for the avalanche which she was sure this fall would cause. After a few seconds, she realized that there was no rumbling sound, and although the snow continued to come down furiously, there was no sudden rush of it.

In the distance she heard a howling noise that could be the wind or—or wolves! She had to move on! Jennifer plunged a pole into the snow and shifted her weight, forcing her body up to a standing position. She had gone only a few feet when she fell still another time. "Why can't you be a better skier?" she scolded herself. "Jarod needs you!"

Another part of herself answered, "I know, but I'm so scared, And this part of the mountain is getting so steep."

Everything was deathly silent. She wished that she could hear Jarod screaming for help. At least then she'd know he could breathe. She rose again to a standing position. She was exhausted. She needed to rest, but she had to get down to Jarod. She couldn't keep falling like this. He needed her now! Finally, she began to carefully sidestep her way down the steepness. It may have been skiing for babies, but Jennifer didn't care. Suddenly, she heard a noise, and she jumped. Another avalanche! She was going to be buried, too! She froze right where she was and waited to be swept away.

When the noise stopped, and she was still standing, Jennifer forced herself to open her eyes. There had been no further avalanche. One of the few trees in the area had broken under the weight of the added snow that had been dumped on it, and she had heard the branches breaking and the rush of their falling snow.

"Move, Jennifer!" she commanded her shaking legs. Her breath was coming in ragged spurts, but she tried to ignore it and push herself closer to the area where she had last seen Jarod. "Jarod!" she shouted. But there was no response.

Jennifer had never felt so alone and so scared in her life. She put her downhill pole into the snow, moved her downhill ski and stepped into the track with her uphill ski. Again and again she did this, moving slowly downward. This time when she put her pole in the snow, she felt it hit something. Oh, no!

she thought, hoping she had not pierced Jarod's head with the sharp tip of her pole.

"Jarod!" she cried, falling to the ground and beginning to dig furiously in the snow. In a matter of seconds, her hand hit something hard, but when she tried to pull the object out, nothing happened. She felt it again. It felt like a rock. Great, she thought. What good does a buried rock do anyone! She was so tired. Her chest hurt. A hundred times, her doctor had told her and her parents that when she felt like this it was important for her to just sit and rest for awhile. But how could she do that? She was all her brother had, and even without resting, she was afraid that she was too little and she was too late to save him.

CHAPTER 6

Suddenly Jennifer heard a terrible kind of moaning. Could it be? She screamed, "Jarod." There was no answer. "Jarod, answer me. Where are you?" she screamed, trying to move in the direction of the noise.

"If only it weren't snowing so hard!" She could barely see anything at all. "You can do this!" she told herself as she tried to ski parallel. She braced her body for another fall, but either the slope's steepness had evened out or the avalanche had taken away the moguls.

"Help me!" Jennifer heard a faint voice.

"I'm coming!" she screamed. "Jarod, I'm coming! Keep talking so I can try to find you!"

"So cold," Jennifer could hear Jarod saying now. "So cold. Can't move." Then moaning began again.

Jennifer kept moving in the direction of Jarod's voice. She tried not to think that this scared, strange voice sounded nothing like her brother. "Please," she prayed, "please just let me get to him fast. Don't let him be hurt, please!"

"I'm coming, Jarod," she yelled again. "I'm almost there!"

"Jen...Jen...Jen..." Jarod called.

Just a few feet in front of Jennifer was a huge mound of snow. "Jarod?" she called.

"Here...I...I must be trapped." Jarod called back.

Jennifer began to sidestep carefully, trying not to hit Jarod with her skis or poles, or end up skiing past him. Then finally, Jarod was right in front of her—or at least the little bit of him there was to see. Only his head and shoulders stuck out from the snow. The rest of his body was buried in white. "But he's alive," Jennifer told herself. "He's alive."

"I'm coming, Jarod. Just hold on!" Yet, even as she said it, Jennifer wondered how anyone could survive very long completely packed in snow.

Directly in front of Jarod now, Jennifer worked quickly to release herself from her skis. Standing them upright, she dropped to her knees to get closer to her buried brother, but without the skis to hold her up, she immediately sank down into the snow up to her hips. Still, she reached out by Jarod's right shoulder and began to dig with her hands as if she were a little puppy. Frantically, she plowed her hands through the snow until more and more of his arm emerged. At last, she had dug down to his hand. Her own hands throbbed with the cold and the struggle. "Jarod," she said, gasping from her effort, "Jarod, we've got your arm free."

Jarod's teeth were chattering. "Huh?" Jennifer began to rub his arm as hard as she could. "Come on, Jarod," she said as much for herself as for him. "Your arm is okay. Lift it up. You can do it. You know you can." Yet the arm did not move, and Jarod gave no sign that he was even trying.

"Jarod!" Jennifer tried to shake his shoulder. "Move your arm," she screamed into his ear. Still nothing. Jennifer rubbed his arm harder. Her hands hurt from from the friction of her mittens against his sleeve. Finally, Jarod slowly raised his arm, hen let it fall. Jennifer gasped, "Oh, thank you! Thank you! Come on, Jarod. Move your arm again. You can do it!"

Jarod lifted his arm and made a face.

"Does it hurt? Does it feel broken?"

"I don't think so." Jarod said uncertainly, "But I'm not sure. It's...it's so cold...I'm not sure if I even feel it at all."

Still, he did seem to be able to pick up and put down his arm. Jennifer sat in the snow to rest and suddenly noticed her own breathing. It was ragged and sounded wheezy. Slipping her inhaler out of her jacket pocket, Jennifer pushed the cap off with the thumb of her glove and took two more sprays. She wasn't supposed to take sprays this close together, but she could feel her chest tightening. She waited a minute, hoping the drug would open her lungs. "You've got to stay calm," the doctor had always told her. "Getting upset when you cannot breathe only makes everything worse. Do not cry. Do not scream. Just stay calm and focus on breathing normally." She could hear the doctor's voice saying every one of those words, but how could he have any idea what it must feel like to be on a deserted mountain in the middle of a huge snow storm and not be breathing right?

"Jarod," Jennifer said between breaths. "You've got to use that arm to help dig the rest of you out. I can't do it by myself. I can't breathe well enough. I've got to rest a minute."

"Right," Jarod said foggily. "You're right." But he still didn't move.

Jennifer crawled over to Jarod. She took her hands and began to rub his cheeks and the top of his head. She rubbed as hard as she could trying to get the circulation going.

Finally, Jarod spoke aloud to himself, saying, "Dig arm, dig arm!" Slowly, he took the right arm that Jennifer had freed and moved it across his body. He began to make efforts to push away the snow that engulfed his left arm. Jennifer crawled around behind him and dug at the back of his arm as Jarod tried to free the front.

Jennifer felt so tired. How could this powdery snow seem so light when it fell on her glove and so heavy when she tried to move it from Jarod's arms? There was a part of her that wished she could just sink down in the snow and rest. It seemed to her that she had been digging forever, but the dumb snow kept falling and falling.

Finally, Jarod's left arm was freed as well. Jarod looked at it. "I can't feel it, Jen! I can't feel it at all," he said in a panicky voice.

Jennifer grabbed the sleeve of his jacket and began to shake the arm back and forth, back and forth. Then Jarod rubbed the front of his left arm with his right and Jennifer rubbed the back until at last, Jarod picked up his arm. "It hurts," he said.

"But you moved it, Jarod. You can move both arms," Jennifer said between gasps.

Jarod crossed his arms across his chest and began to pound each mittened hand against the opposite arm. "Ya-ya-you rest." Jarod's teeth were chattering. "I'll start digging out my legs."

At least the snow was not packed in hard. As Jennifer rested, that was about the only good thing she could think of. As for bad things, there were too many to count. The snow kept falling. No one knew they were here. They were completely alone. She could barely breathe. There might be more snowslides or wild animals waiting for them.

Jennifer rested a minute more until the worst of the aching in her chest stopped. She tried not to think how bad things could be. It was too scary. She leaned over to help Jarod dig at his legs. Yet she had barely begun before she felt as if her own hands had completely frozen.

"The poles," Jarod said. "Let's try to use them." Jennifer took one pole and gave Jarod the other, and the two of them tried using the pointed end first and then switched to the handled end to clear the snow from Jarod's legs.

It may have been minutes or hours, for it was impossible to tell how much time passed on the mountain, but finally, Jarod was free. Shivering, he grabbed Jennifer and hugged her tightly. "I'm okay," he told them both. "I'm going to be okay."

While Jennifer hugged him back, she could almost feel the cold of his body. She fought back tears. "I'm glad you're okay. It was pretty scary to hear that snow start to rumble. I couldn't even see for sure whether you were in it or had gotten down below it." She started to sniffle. "Then I heard this noise. I thought it was wolves..."

Jarod interrupted. "Jen, let's not worry about all that. It's over. We're going to be okay. That's what we have to think now." He tried to stand up, but felt as if he was going to fall over. Finally, he managed to stand and then jump around to warm his legs. The more he moved, the more his head cleared. He looked at the changed mountain around them and shuddered. What if he had twisted and landed head down instead of up?

He made himself stop thinking about anything bad that might have happened. Instead, he forced himself to try to concentrate on what they should do next. He looked at his sister. "We're okay. We just have to figure out how to get out of here."

He held up his tan knit hat. They had found it while digging out his left hand. "I think I remember Mrs. Foster saying in science that a lot of heat escapes from your head, so it's important to keep your head covered in the cold, but I don't know about this hat." He tried to brush off the encrusted snow. "It's pretty messed up."

"Your ears look purple." Jennifer said. "Try to shake off more of the snow and put the hat on way down over your ears."

Jarod pulled the knit hat onto his head and down over his ears. He shuddered. It was like putting an icicle on his head.

"I wish it would stop snowing so hard," Jennifer said.

"That's actually good," Jarod said. "If it gets too cold, it won't snow. Since it's snowing so hard, it's not as cold."

That sounded crazy to Jennifer, but she didn't argue. Whether it made it warmer or not, the huge, falling snowflakes made it impossible to see more than a few inches in front of them.

"Put your skis back on, and let's get out of here before it gets darker," Jarod ordered.

"All right," Jennifer said. She stared out at the sky. She hadn't noticed until now, but it was definitely getting darker. Jennifer shivered from the idea of being out here all alone at night, or maybe she shivered from the cold she felt now, or maybe she shivered for both reasons. Using the point of her ski pole, she tried to scrape the snow from the bottom of her boots so that her boots would fit into her ski bindings. It wasn't going to be easy to get her skis back on without being on a flat place. She tried to lean into her uphill ski to put them on.

Just as she got her left foot into its binding, Jarod yelled, "I don't believe it," and dropped to his knees.

Jennifer was almost afraid to ask. What else could possibly go wrong? she wondered. Jarod had begun digging around in the snow. "What are you looking for?" she asked. "I think we should go before it gets darker."

"Right," Jarod said, and he coughed like he was going to cry but was trying not to. He kept trying to push snow away from one spot and then another around the place he had been buried. "There's just one problem. My snowboard. I thought it must be right here. At first, I didn't realize that it had come off my feet. Then when you got me free, and I saw it was missing, I thought the snowboard must be right next to me. I mean, my hat was right here. How could a big thing like my snowboard be missing? I had the leash on."

It seemed to Jennifer that it was getting darker by the minute. "Jarod, please, let's forget about the snowboard. Let's just get to the bottom of the slope."

Jarod pounded his hands against his arms, still trying to warm them. "Jennifer, don't you get it? How am I going to get down this slope without my snowboard? Every time I take a step, I'm going to sink down in the snow. Can't you see? Without my snowboard, I can't get down to the bottom before it's totally dark. That's why we've got to find my board."

Jarod began digging again, but there was so much snow around them. How far had he been dragged from the top of the snowslide? Jarod wondered. Even he didn't know for sure. He looked up at Jennifer. "It's bright blue. How could it be lost in all this white? My board just can't be that hard to find!"

Jennifer went to take her skis off again, but instead they sort of took off with her on them. Suddenly, she was a ways below Jarod, and she found herself carefully sidestepping back up to try to reach him. Her legs ached.

"Gee, what are you doing!" he yelled as she climbed back up to him. "I say I need help, and you take off!"

"I didn't mean to," Jennifer said. "My skis just went."

Jarod looked at her. Her face was almost as bright a pink as her ski outfit. "I wish there was a way for me to make your skis stay on my boots. Then maybe I could just carry you or something."

Jennifer shook her head. "I don't see how that would work." She shoved her uphill pole into the ground hard to get ready to take off her skis. "Jarod, I think my pole hit something!" Jennifer pulled her skis off without removing the pole, then dropped to her knees to dig around it. "It felt hard," she said, "I think it might be your snowboard!" She brushed away more snow, and her hand hit the hardness.

Jarod scrambled over to where Jennifer was. "Jennifer, I think you really saved us. As soon as I get my snowboard back on... " He stopped midsentence when Jennifer held up the hard thing her pole had hit...a tree branch.

"I...I'm sorry, Jarod," she said. "I don't know how a tree branch got here. I thought it was your board. I guess the snow must have moved a lot of stuff." Jennifer felt tired and hot and cold at the same time. How would they ever get out of this?

"Jarod, there's a whole mountain around us. I don't know how we'll ever find your snowboard. Can't you make some skis out of this branch?"

Jarod's own fear caused him to scream, "Jennifer, that's the dumbest idea I've ever heard! Only an idiot would think of that. It's just great that I'm stuck up here with my stupid little sister."

"Oh, yeah?" Jennifer cried. "I don't care what you say! I may be scared, and I may not know what to do here, but I'm not stupid. And you should say you're sorry!"

The two of them glared at each other, and then both heard another rumbling sound.

CHAPTER 7

They turned their heads toward the sound of the rumble and saw off to the far right another snowslide hurtling down from what looked like a cliff. When the sound stopped, both were still frozen to the spot. Finally, Jennifer stuttered, "Do...do...do you think there might still be more of those avalanches coming?"

Jarod wasn't sure. He'd never seen anything like this before when he'd been snowboarding, but then he'd never gone out of bounds before either. How he wished he had never mouthed off to Eric. The jerk was probably sitting in the ski lodge drinking hot chocolate and harassing some little kid, while he and his sister were up here worried about being buried alive in snow.

Jarod shook his head. He'd been so sure that they'd gotten the last laugh on that jerk. He looked at Jennifer. She looked so scared. This was all his fault. Some big brother he'd turned out to be. At least he could try to make her think things weren't as bad as he knew they were.

Trying to sound convincing, he said "Actually, Jen, I think I read that usually there's a second slide after the first, and that's it. So I think we're safe. We found my hat, so my board must be right around here. I'll find it pretty soon, and then we'll get out of here. Hey, we'll still be back in time for dinner." He forced his voice to sound normal. "I get dibs on the first hot shower when we get back to the hotel."

He clamped his mouth shut so that his teeth couldn't chatter. Neither one spoke as they used Jennifer's poles to sweep through the snow around them.

"Wait! I feel something!" Jarod cried. He dug faster with the handle of the pole and then reached down into the snow. It seemed like the blue of the snowboard should be showing by now, but it wasn't. As he reached for the object that the pole kept hitting, he worried that it was only another tree branch. Instead, his hand grasped the nylon of the tan backpack. He had forgotten all about it.

Jennifer bit her lip. Her mother had given them that backpack just a few hours ago, but it seemed like that had been a very long time back. Jarod looked at his sister fighting back tears. "Hey," he said, "I'll bet there'll be things in this that will help us warm up." Jarod grabbed the zipper and yanked, but the zipper seemed frozen. When he looked up from trying to move it, he realized that although the snow had stopped falling so hard, the light was growing dimmer and dimmer. Soon they wouldn't be able to see at all. The backpack would have to wait. They had to find his snowboard, and they had to find it now! Jarod looked out at all the white around him. The board could be anywhere! Overwhelmed, he stopped digging.

Just then, Jennifer called. "My pole—I hit something. Come here!" Jarod forced his stiffening legs to walk toward her. With each step, he sank into the snow. "I see blue!" Jennifer called. "I think this might be it!"

In spite of his exhaustion, Jarod felt his heart start to pound.

Maybe there was hope after all. If he could just get the snowboard back on, at least they could keep moving downhill before it was totally dark. Jarod moved right next to Jennifer and started furiously digging with her. She was right! He could see the blue of the board himself, and soon, he was pulling it out of the snow. Never had anything looked so good. He used Jennifer's pole to clean off the bottom of one foot to put into the board's bindings, but his foot wouldn't stay in. Then he looked again. Both bindings were broken. The board must have hit something after it had come off his feet. He clapped his hands together to try to warm them while he thought. What good was a snowboard if he couldn't keep it on his feet?

"Come on," Jennifer said. "I'm so cold. Let's go."

Jarod bit his lip, but he couldn't feel it. "Jen, my board is broken. I can't keep it on my feet."

Jennifer pushed her goggles up on her head, and her eyes held terror in them as they looked at Jarod.

He looked over at the backpack. "If I can just get the backpack open, maybe there's something in there that I can use to keep my snowboard on." Jennifer nodded mutely and watched Jarod strain at the zipper. Each unsuccessful tug made their plight seem even worse to her. Finally, Jarod looked up, "It's no use." Seeing his sister's face, he added quickly, "But I'll think of something else."

Jarod looked around. There was nothing that could possibly keep a snowboard attached to his boots. Then Jarod glanced down and noticed the cord in the bottom of his jacket. "Jen, I think I can just tie my board on with this cord. It'll be okay." The first two times he grabbed the cord, his hand was so stiff that the cord slipped right through them. Finally, after sliding and pulling at it a little at a time, he managed to get the cord out of his jacket. Wrapping it around both hands and pulling, he decided that although it wasn't as long as he would have liked it to be, it seemed pretty strong. It would have to do. It was all he had.

Cleaning off the snow from his boot once again, he put his foot on the board and bent to slip the cord through the binding and over the top of his foot. He barely had enough cord to tie a square knot. He'd just have to balance his back foot on the board without any binding.

Jennifer watched Jarod struggling with his snowboard. She saw that his face was set in concentration, but there was a look of fear in his eyes. She realized that Jarod was as scared as she was. That was when she decided to be even braver for him.

"Hey, I put my skis on while you were fixing the board. I bet that we're closer to the bottom than we think. Besides, it's stopped snowing now. That's a good sign, huh?" Jennifer hoped her voice sounded cheerier than she felt.

"You're right, Jen. After all, we were partway down the mountain before we ever went off Sunday Stroll. We're probably almost down to the bottom now." Jarod wondered if Jennifer believed his lies any more than he believed hers.

Though the snow had stopped falling, it was getting so dark that Jarod could barely see his sister two feet in front of him. "You start now and get a little head start since you're a slower skier."

Jennifer nodded. Her whole body was shaking. She put her skis together and began to move down the slope. Trying to balance his weight carefully, Jarod hoped he could stay on his board. "Hey," he told himself out loud. "It's just like surfing. Those guys don't have bindings on their boards, and they stay on." He tried to move as carefully as he could, and to his surprise, he found himself still upright as he headed downward. Then suddenly, he felt the board hit a mogul. He tried to grip his toes down in his boot to hang on, but the board bounced and his foot slipped right off of the board, which kept going down the slope. "Jennifer!" he screamed. "My board...see if you can catch my board. It's heading down."

He couldn't see exactly where the board was going, and in the darkness he could barely see Jennifer, but he hoped that somehow she could stop his board. Too tired to walk, he sat down and tried to push himself downward on his backside. It was not fast going. While the board had skimmed across the top of the snow, Jarod was not so lucky. He sank into powdery whiteness and had to keep pushing with his hands to propel himself. "I don't see your snowboard," Jennifer called. "What happened to it? Are you all right?"

Her voice sounded a little faint, and before he could answer, he heard a piercing scream. What now? he thought. What else is left to go wrong?

"Jennifer" he called. "Answer me. What happened to you?"

But there was no response. Jarod forced himself to try to slide faster. His entire backside was practically numb, but he told himself that he couldn't think about that now. He had to find Jennifer.

"Push!" he told himself. "Push yourself." He plunged his hands back into the snow and tried to force his body to move faster. Then all of a sudden, he felt himself in the air. He screamed and landed with a thud.

"Jarod?" came a voice close to him.

"What happened?" Jarod asked.

"It's getting so dark that it's hard to see, but I think there must be a cliff or a ledge or something there. You can't really tell when you're above it, but then everything just drops out. I fell. My skis came off."

It felt to Jarod as if not only his knees and hands but even his heart was shaking. "Um...did you see my snowboard? It came off my feet. The cord didn't hold."

"I found my skis. I have them both now."

"Jen...my board!" Jarod shouted. "Aren't you listening? What about it?"

"It's...it's." There was a catch in her voice. "It's here—sort of." She had moved closer to Jarod. In her hands, she held two jagged pieces of wood. "I'm sorry."

Jarod ran his glove over the edge of the broken board. It certainly wasn't going to take him or anyone else anywhere ever again. Jennifer was crying softly. "I wish I could see Mommy and Daddy one more time to tell them I love them."

Jarod commanded, "Jennifer, stop that! We are going to see Mom and Dad lots more times."

Jennifer lifted the goggles that had been protecting her eyes and felt the sting of the icy air. She looked at Jarod. "No, we're not," she said. "I'm not a baby. The truth is that it's nighttime. We have no idea where we are. My hands already feel like blocks of ice, and your snowboard is all broken." There was a long pause, and then she continued softly, "I don't see how we can stay alive."

Jarod folded his arms across his chest and pounded his hands on his arms. They couldn't just give up. There had to be something. "Jennifer, we just have to think. We can do it. If we can just get through tonight, as soon as we can see, we can either make it to the bottom ourselves or rescuers will find us. You know that by now Mom probably has the entire state looking for us up here. It's just one night, Jen. We can do that!"

But as he said the words, Jarod wondered how that was possible. Even his breath seemed to freeze in the air when he spoke. There wasn't any place to get shelter, the trees had disappeared from this area, and the wind was starting to blow. He tried as hard as he could to think if he had ever learned anything in school or from television or books about how people had survived in this kind of arctic weather, but nothing came.

Then, in the back of his mind came pieces of some story his class had read earlier in the year. It had been about some guys who got lost hiking in Alaska. "Think," he told himself. "What did they do?" He hadn't been paying real close attention because they'd read the story during football season. He remembered Mrs. Peck had interrupted his daydream of playing for the Cardinals by saying, "So, Jarod, how do you think these men built the snow cave?"

"I don't know," he'd replied. And when some kids had laughed, he'd added, "I don't think we'll need any snow caves in Phoenix."

He sure wished he'd paid attention now, but somehow he and Jen would have to figure it out. They could make shelter. They would build a snow cave and get out of the wind and wait until morning. How to do it, he wasn't sure, but he and

Jen had built igloos out of snow when they lived in Denver. Maybe it was kind of the same thing.

"Jennifer, I have an idea. Give me a piece of my broken snowboard," Jarod ordered.

"You can't try to still go anywhere on it. It's too messed up," Jennifer said in a flat voice.

"Jen, I'm not going to board on it. I'm going to use it to help dig us a snow cave. You know, bears spend whole winters in caves, and they come out fine. We're going to build a cave for us for one night, and we'll be fine, too."

"I can't," Jennifer mumbled. "I'm too tired and too freezing, and..."

Jarod reached over, grabbed the board, and tapped it lightly against Jennifer's back several times. Finally, she yelled, "Ouch! Cut it out!"

"That's better," Jarod said. "Don't give up. We're going to make it! Now, come on. I need some help!"

Jarod looked at the ledge from which they had fallen. It curved inward underneath. He decided that was good because they would be more protected. And he wondered if they could tunnel into the area underneath the ledge. That would be easier than trying to build a whole igloo out here. But what would happen if they tried to dig in under the ledge? Would snow collapse around them? He took the piece of snowboard and shoved it into the snow under the ledge. Using his piece of snowboard as a shovel, Jarod scooped out more and more snow. Once he had a pile, he began to shape it into walls.

Jennifer had begun to help him. The two worked in silence, and the only sounds were those of the snowboards scraping the snow away. It was hard to be so tired and so cold and to still keep working, but the other choice was so awful that they kept working anyway. Jarod told himself, "Just keep thinking, one more pile of snow. One more pile of snow."

Jennifer thought of nothing at all. Part of her just wanted to lie down here and go to sleep. The other part of her said that if Jarod could keep hoping, so could she, so she forced herself to push away another pile of snow.

Neither of them had any idea of how long they had been working. Darkness had covered the ski slopes, and the heavy clouds obscured any stars. The snow had begun blowing around them. Finally, Jennifer said, "I'm too tired and cold to dig any more. Let's see if we can get in."

"Okay," Jarod replied. "You first." Jennifer crawled through the narrow entrance and found a place to sit. "I'm here," she called. "Are you coming?" Jarod crawled in, relieved to find that they both fit inside the cave.

Feeling a surge of adrenaline at their accomplishment, Jarod said, "We did it, and, Jennifer, somehow, we're going to do the rest of it, too! Besides, we're going to have the best rescue stories to tell, which reminds me..." He stopped midsentence and forced himself to crawl back out of the cave into the blowing snow. There he took Jennifer's skis and stood them upright, then crossed them in the universal sign for distress. How many times had he seen hurt skiers on the ski slopes with their skis crossed like that waiting for the ski patrol? If there were helicopters out looking tonight, maybe they would see the skis from the air! He hoped so with all his heart.

Jarod took two pieces of the snowboard and crawled back

into the cave with them. "Here," he said. "We need to sit on these so we're not right on the snow."

It was so dark in the cave that he fell over Jennifer. "We fit before. Move your legs," he said.

"I can't," Jennifer replied. "I've got the backpack between them. I keep thinking there's got to be something in it that can help us. Mom was so determined that you take it for me. I'm trying to work on the zipper. When I keep rubbing it with my gloves, it moves a little bit."

"That's good, Jen!" Somehow, Jarod wedged his own body next to hers. "Let me try now." He reached his hand over and felt for the bag and its zipper. Tugging harder, he found that Jennifer had moved the zipper a little bit. "Come on," he talked aloud to it. "Open up! We need a little luck from something."

CHAPTER 8

Jarod tugged and tugged until the zipper finally pulled, and the bag opened. "We did it!" he shouted.

"What's in there?" Jennifer asked. "Anything warm?"

It was too dark to see what was in the bag, so Jarod tried lifting something out, then trying to feel through his gloves what it was. "This is small. It's hard. It feels sort of familiar, but I can't quite think what it is."

"Let me feel," Jennifer said excitedly. "I just know it's going to be something really good." Jarod told her to cup her hands in front of her, and reaching to feel them, he dumped the object into her hands.

"Got it?" he asked.

"Yes, it's...it's...another inhaler." The disappointment in her voice was obvious.

Trying somehow to keep their spirits up, he said, "Hey, it's only the first thing. There's got to be a lot more. Mom wouldn't have given me a whole backpack that she said was to take care of you if she only wanted to put in an extra inhaler."

Jennifer didn't say anything. Inside her mittens, she crossed her icy fingers and hoped that somehow their mom had packed food and warm clothes, blankets, and maybe even a cell phone.

"Okay, Jen, I'm going to try again," Jarod said, knowing

that she couldn't see what he was doing. He reached his hand into the bag once more and tried to feel the objects. It was like that old birthday party game they used to play where everyone got to put their hands into a paper sack and try to guess the objects inside. The one who came the closest got the prize. Only this time, he wasn't playing for prizes, and it didn't really matter whether he guessed the objects correctly or not. If there wasn't something to help them keep warm...Jarod stopped himself from finishing the thought. It was just too terrible.

He pulled another object out of the bag and began feeling it. It was hard to determine what anything really felt like with these heavy gloves on, but he knew better than to take them off even for a few minutes. Even with the gloves on, his fingers alternated between feeling numb and having stabbing little needles in them. Yet, through his gloves, he continued to make his unwilling fingers poke and prod at this newest object. Then all of a sudden, his eyes closed at a blinding light. Oh, no, he thought. What now?

"You did it! Oh, Jarod! It feels so much better not to be in the dark!" Jennifer clapped her hands. "Doesn't it seem better! Quit pointing that thing in your eyes, and let's use it to see what else is in the bag." Jennifer pushed his arm, and the light moved away from blinding him. He opened his eyes and saw the silver flashlight. Though not very large, it gave a strong, bright beam of light.

"Wow! Who'd have thought we'd ever need a flashlight? I wonder how Mom ever knew to put one in!" Jarod said in amazement.

"I don't know. Maybe it was just left in the backpack from

the last time you went camping. I don't care. I'm just so glad it's there. It's better that it's not so dark in here, huh?" Jennifer's stomach made a loud grumbling noise. "I guess it's been kind of a long time since we ate. Maybe there's food in the bag, too. You know how Mom likes to make sure I eat enough. I hope she was thinking about that when she packed this backpack. You want me to hold the flashlight or take the stuff out of the pack?"

"Doesn't matter," said Jarod. Part of him couldn't wait to get to everything in the bag, and part of him didn't want to take anything else out. The contents of this bag were all they had. Until they saw everything, they could always hope. Jennifer must have felt the same way because both of them sat for a second, not moving toward the bag's objects. Finally, Jennifer told him, "I'll hold the flashlight. You can take the stuff out."

"Okay." Jarod reached into the bag and found a little foil container. "What is this? Shine the flashlight closer so I can read it."

Jennifer did, and Jarod read, "Handwarmer. Break the seal and place inside glove or sock for twenty minutes to warm hand or foot." Just reading the words made Jarod realize how cold his hands and feet felt.

"We...uh...we could pass it back and forth," Jennifer suggested.

Reluctantly, Jarod put the handwarmer down without opening it. "Let's look at everything we've got, and then we'll decide how to use each thing the best."

Jennifer nodded. The next thing he drew out was a small

thermos. Jennifer and Jarod gasped at the same time. "Open it!" Jennifer called. And then she continued half to herself, "Oh, please be something very hot!"

Jarod struggled with the plastic cup lid and finally got it off. Even harder was getting his bulky gloves to unscrew the inside lid, but finally, the lid came off. He immediately put his face close to the top and felt the warmth rise toward his nose. Face still next to the opening, he meant to move away and put the lid back on to keep the liquid hot, but suddenly, he found himself taking a swig. His mouth was filled with warmth, and he could feel it begin to slide down his throat. Never had anything tasted or felt so good. He started to tip the thermos to his lips again, when Jennifer called, "Wait! I want some, too."

"Sorry, Jen. I didn't mean to take any. It was just that it was so close, and it smelled so good, and I was so cold. I really am sorry. Why don't you take a drink, too, and then we'll put the lid on until we have everything and we can plan how to use it."

He handed Jennifer the thermos, but it slipped from her hands. She screamed as she saw it start to fall, and Jarod realized that the warm liquid was about to spill. He cupped his hands under the thermos and caught it before it hit the ground. A little had sloshed out, but the spill wasn't nearly as bad as it could have been.

Jennifer was crying. "How could I have done that?"

"Hey, it's okay. Your hands are just real cold. I'll hold it, and you drink. You'll feel better after you do."

Jennifer took a small sip of the liquid. "It's chicken soup!" she said in delight. "Can I have one more sip?"

Jarod gave her another sip, and both of them watched solemnly as he screwed the inner lid back on the thermos. It was all he could do to keep himself from gulping the whole thing down. Their eyes stayed on the thermos for a good minute after it was capped. "That was so good," Jennifer said.

Jarod nodded. "I thought it would be hot chocolate, but this was even better."

"I can't have the hot chocolate because I'm not supposed to have too much milk," Jennifer said, her eyes still riveted on the thermos.

Jarod shook his head and broke the trance they both seemed to be in. "Let's get the rest of this unpacked." *Come on, Mom!* he silently prayed. *Please have filled this thing with the stuff we'll need.* He pulled out a pink knit hat, an extra pair of socks, a pink fleece muffler, and two more hand warmer kits. Finally, there were two little packages about three inches square. Both said, "Miracle Blanket! This thin mylar blanket can be placed over shoulders or lap to keep you warm while watching the coldest football games." At the bottom of the bag was a piece of lined paper that was folded and said, "Jarod and Jennifer," written in scrolling lavender ink.

Jarod unfolded the note. "'Dear Kids,'" he read aloud. His voice was kind of husky.

"Are you crying?" Jennifer asked. 'Cause I feel like it, and you sound like it."

"I'm not crying. It's just that my voice is cold," he lied. Then he continued reading aloud. "'I hope you both are having a wonderful afternoon together. Jen, sweetheart, don't let your-self get too cold or too tired. I've put lots of things in to help keep you warm. Remember that you don't want to get sick.'"

Jarod paused, then continued to read, "'The man in the sporting goods store said that the miracle blankets are great to use on the chairlifts. They fold up real small, so you can just tuck them back into the backpack when you're ready to ski. I love you both! Mom'"

There was a P.S. attached at the bottom. "'Jarod, thanks for being such a good big brother to Jen. Tonight, you can pick where we go to dinner.'"

Jennifer was making hiccoughing, crying sounds. Jarod felt like joining her. More than anything he wished he was back with his parents right now. This all seemed so impossible. He could feel his eyes start to sting. "Toughen up!" he told himself. If he didn't stay really strong, he knew he'd kill himself and his little sister.

Aloud he said, "Jen, don't cry! We're going to see Mom tomorrow." He tried to joke. "And don't think that you get to pick the restaurant tomorrow night. It'll still be my turn since I missed tonight!" Jennifer continued to sob softly.

"Hey, if you keep crying, it's just going to start your asthma. So just stop! We have to figure out how we want to use this stuff, and I need your help, okay?"

"Okay," Jen said still sniffling.

"All right, then. I think we should sit on one of these miracle blanket things and wrap it around our legs. We can put it on top of the snowboards but under our butts. Okay? And we'll put the other miracle blanket around our backs." He held up the pink knit hat. "Here, put this on under your black hat. It will help keep your head warmer."

She shook her head. "No, you take this one. Your hat is all wet. I'll be okay. Like you said, we both have to help. I can take my hair out of the ponytail. My hair will cover my ears and help keep them warm."

Jarod didn't argue. He pulled off his damp tan hat and rubbed his ears hard, but he couldn't get any feeling back in them. Finally, he shrugged and pulled on the dry hat, hoping its warmth would restore some feeling in his ears.

Jennifer shined the flashlight on him. She gave a weak smile. "I never thought I'd see you in bright pink!"

Jarod tried to smile back. "Yeah, my newest best color." Next he held up the socks. "I think that if I take off my boots, I'll never get them on again. What about you?"

Jennifer shook her head. "I can't even think about getting mine off."

Jarod looked at the socks. "Put them on under your mittens. They'll be like inside gloves."

"But what about you?"

"Jen, just do it! You know your gloves have to be wet from all the digging you did. Get your fingers warmed up!"

Jennifer didn't move. She still held the flashlight in one hand. Jarod reached over roughly and pulled at the other mitten until he had it off her hand. Then using both of his hands, he pulled the sock onto her hand and began rubbing it hard with both of his hands. She cried out in pain as tingles of sharp needles went through her fingers. "That's good," Jarod said. "That means you're getting your circulation going." He didn't know if that was true or not, but he did know that the socks would help.

"Wait, Jarod...I have an idea. I'll put the other sock on my hand, but you put your hand in it, too. Then we can wrap it in the plastic wrapper from the miracle blanket and that will keep the sock dry. Besides, then when we use the hand warmer, we can use one for two of us."

Jarod looked at his sister. Sometimes she was a pretty smart kid. He remembered when they had been camping that someone had said that when it got real cold, people shared sleeping bags because shared body heat kept them warmer. So it made sense that maybe their hands would share heat if they were right next to each other. Besides, his fingers were so cold that he felt he'd better do something or he was going to lose the use of them. "Good idea, Jen. Let's get everything else just the way we want it, and then we'll get our hands fixed last."

"Let's stuff our empty backpack down by the opening to try to block out cold air coming into the cave. We don't really need it now that it's empty, do we?" Jen asked. "Can't hurt." Jarod answered. "Let me just check inside it one more time first." Although he hoped he had missed something, the bag seemed to be empty. Just to make sure, he turned it upside down and shook it. Nothing came out, but he heard something rattling. Then he remembered the extra zippered pocket in the back of the bag. How could he have forgotten that!

The zipper pulled open without too much effort. Jarod dug inside and pulled out a Milky Way, a Hershey's chocolate bar, and four cherry granola bars. His heart lifted. "Reservation for two for dinner coming up!" he said to Jennifer.

He waved the candy under her eyes. In what he hoped was a French accent, he said, "Voud Madame vant ze chef's special of chocolatte or voud she prefer ze house favorite of ze cherrie?"

Jennifer managed a smile. "Your French is awful, but I could eat both!"

Jarod sighed, "Me, too. But I don't think we should. Let's space the food out in case we need it tomorrow to get more energy before we get rescued."

Jennifer thought to herself, *If* we get rescued. But she didn't say anything because she realized Jarod was trying so hard to be brave for both of them. Meanwhile, Jarod had unwrapped both of the Miracle Blankets. They opened up to pretty big squares of a kind of heavy silvery mylar stuff. As tightly as Jarod and Jennifer were wedged into the cave, it wasn't going to be easy getting one of these blankets under themselves and around their legs.

"Okay," Jarod said, "I'll lift up a little and slide this thing under it." He put his hands down on the snowboard and tried to raise himself off the ground. "Ouch!" he called, as his head bumped the top of the snow cave. A little snow came loose and fell on his lap.

Jennifer shined the light up toward the top of the cave. "Do you think this whole thing could just collapse on us?"

Jarod shuddered. "Let's say no because I don't want to think about yes."

Then he caught a glimpse of the fear in Jennifer's eyes. "Hey, we dug the snow out from under a ledge. Even if the roof fell in a little, there are big rocks up above. It's not like we would get buried in snow."

Jennifer nodded her head solemnly. "Yeah, I didn't think about that." Jarod had no idea if what he had said was true, but it at least made Jennifer a little less afraid. Besides, he really did think they'd packed the snow real tight, and it was so cold that nothing should melt. He glanced up to the snow roof and shuddered. It was just too awful to think about being suffocated by the roof collapsing. "Here," he said to Jennifer. "Let me hold the flashlight. You try to get this thing under you. You're not as tall as I am, so you probably won't hit the top if you're careful."

Jarod took the flashlight, and Jennifer maneuvered and squirmed until she had the mylar blanket under her. Her left leg was wedged right against Jarod's right leg, and when they pulled the mylar blanket up around their legs, it completely covered them. "Well, step one went okay," Jarod said. "Now for step two." He handed Jennifer the flashlight and tried to lean forward enough to squeeze the mylar between the back of his jacket and the back wall of their snow cave. As he struggled with it, he couldn't help wondering how this thin piece of stuff was going to keep them warm, but it was all they had. Jennifer reached behind him and tried to help pull the mylar. Then they switched and Jennifer scooted the mylar blanket behind her back. Together, they pulled the two ends of the blanket around the front of them, and though it didn't completely close, it was pretty close.

Jennifer was the first to speak. "It doesn't feel quite like a real blanket, huh?"

Jarod sighed, "No. It probably just takes a while to work. Besides, real blankets never would have fit in the backpack. The mylar is probably like stuff they use in space—small so it could fit, but designed to do a big job. Hey, if it could keep astronauts safe millions of miles from earth, it's got to work here on a ski slope."

There was a note of hope in Jennifer's voice as she said, "You know, Mrs. Johnson was telling us about a lot of important stuff that we have because of exploring space, but she never talked about this. I'll have to tell her how one thin little piece of mylar that they use for space travel worked like a thick blanket for us."

Jarod thought to himself that he didn't know where he had come up with all this stuff about the blanket being used in space. He'd never seen one before, but it sounded good. He eyed the handwarmers. He wanted to grab them, open them all, and try to warm himself, but he fought the urge. They only had four, and each one was supposed to last about twenty minutes. He knew he'd better wait. The night was only beginning. He and Jennifer would share them equally. The food and chicken soup, too. They'd have to make it last.

He felt Jennifer nudging him. "My face is so freezing. Let's use the muffler to cover our necks and chins."

"Good idea," Jarod said. He'd almost forgotten about the pink muffler. "Tell you what. Let's each take a couple more sips of chicken soup, and we'll each eat a granola bar. Then we can put the muffler on."

Jarod felt his hands and arms shake as he opened the thermos. For a minute or two he just held it up to his lips, feeling the warmth surround them. Finally, he took a sip, and as anxious as he was to swallow it, he held it in his mouth and swirled it around trying to warm his inner cheeks, his tongue, and even his teeth. As the liquid went down his throat, he chewed the noodles and small pieces of chicken, thinking he had never tasted anything as good. He looked at his sister, and for one terrible moment he almost caught himself thinking that he could drink the entire thermos right now. What could Jennifer do about it? Ashamed, he pulled the thermos from his lips and said, "Okay, it's your turn. You take a sip, and then I'll take another and you can take another, and then we'll save the rest for awhile." He told her how to let the open thermos warm her lips first and how to swirl the soup around in her mouth before she swallowed. She went to take the thermos from him, but he said, "I'll hold on to it, too. Your hands are smaller, and we just can't let it drop."

Jennifer nodded. "My mouth is so cold. I don't think I'll even feel the soup."

"You will," Jarod said. He held the thermos up to her lips and heard her groan with pleasure as the warmth hit them. "Okay, Jen, time to take a sip now." Holding the flashlight still with one hand, she put her other hand on the thermos and tilted it toward her. Greedily, she began to gulp the life-giving liquid. Jarod grabbed the thermos from her lips and spilled a little. Both children looked at the spot on the snow where the soup had spilled. "I...I'm so sorry," Jennifer started to cry. "I didn't mean to keep drinking. It just tasted so good. I'm so, so sorry." Her sobs continued.

Part of him was so mad he wanted to hit her. Twice now, it had been her fault they'd wasted part of the only warm liquid they had. But the other part of him knew that she hadn't done it on purpose. He could hear her continue to cry, and wedged too tightly next to her, he could feel her body shake. Jarod picked up one of the granola bars. He tried to open his granola bar with his gloves, but it was impossible. He tore at the foil, but it stayed firmly on the bar. Finally he lifted it to his teeth, put the end of the foil in his mouth, and ripped until he heard the foil give way. Once it was open, he handed the granola bar to Jennifer. "Here. Stop crying. You were just really hungry. You didn't mean anything. Eat this. It will help."

Jennifer reached her hand out from under the mylar shawl. "You're the best big brother. I'm so sorry."

"Jen, forget it. Just eat." Jarod reached for another granola bar for himself and thought bitterly, *the best big brother.* That was a joke. They were only in this mess because of him. Who was it who had said that going off the regular slope would solve all their problems? Who was it who had gotten buried by a snowslide? And who was it who had a broken snowboard?

Jarod continued to beat himself up mentally. And he wondered why he hadn't been able to get them to the bottom of the mountain? They hadn't been that far from it when they had left Sunday Stroll, and they had skied for a while before all this had happened. He began to think and rethink that question. The only thing that made sense was that first it had been snowing too hard, and then it had gotten too dark to see how close to the bottom they really were. But in the morning, it would be clear, and there would be light to see. And somehow, even with the broken snowboard, if they could just see the bottom, Jarod knew they could get there. In fact, all they had to do was to get near people. Then anyone could get them help, and with help, they would finally be warm. Jarod told himself that he was not just wishing for the impossible. As soon as they could see, they could find safety.

Tearing open the second granola bar with his teeth, Jarod thought that everything really would be all right if only they could stay warm enough to make it through this freezing cold and terrifying night.

CHAPTER 9

"**T**he granola bar is kind of frozen, so it takes a long time to chew, but that's probably good. It'll make it last longer, huh?" Without waiting for an answer, Jennifer continued, "Remember how when Mom went on that diet, she was supposed to chew everything fifty times before she swallowed it. The diet book person said that would make her feel not so hungry even if she ate less food."

Jennifer smiled, "You know what? I used to help her count to fifty. If no one else was at the table, we always counted out loud. I think that's why I was the fastest counter in the first grade, but I never told my teacher that."

"Uh-huh," Jarod said with a mouthful of granola bar. Conversation stopped as both of them chewed. It was so quiet that Jarod could almost hear Jennifer's jaws working at the granola bar. When she had finished the last piece, she licked her tongue around the insides of her cheeks and across her teeth, making sure she got every last bit. Then she said, "Jarod, don't get mad, but maybe we could eat one of the candy bars right now, too. I didn't know I was so hungry until I started to eat."

Jarod had to agree with her about feeling hungry. He didn't even like cherry, and this granola bar had not only been cherry but half frozen, too. Still, he thought it had tasted absolutely wonderful. Jennifer was right. Until they'd started eating, they'd been too busy with getting him unburied and trying to find their stuff and building a shelter to think about how hungry they might be. He looked at the candy bars. "Good thing we found this backpack. What if it had stayed lost in the snow?"

Jennifer also eyed the candy bars. "That would have been awful."

Jarod said to himself, "Good ol' Mom." He remembered how angry he'd been when his mother had handed him the backpack to carry for Jennifer. Now he only wished it had contained even more things. Still staring at the candy bars, he felt his mouth water, and he tried to decide if they should save them. "Hmm," he said aloud. "If we're already pretty close to the bottom, we should be able to make it down after it gets light. So we don't have to worry about having to make this food last for a long time..."

"Are we close to the bottom? Do you know that?" Jennifer interrupted.

Jarod didn't know for sure, but he said, "We have to be. It just makes sense. When we left Sunday Stroll, we were already more than halfway down, and we kept going downhill after we went out on our own. I'll bet we could have even seen the bottom from here if it hadn't been snowing so hard and then gotten so dark so fast."

Jennifer sighed. "I sure wish I could have seen the bottom before it got too dark." She squirmed impatiently. "I just wish it would be morning right now."

"Tell you what," Jarod said. "We can split one of the candy bars. I'm sure you can have just a little milk now. You choose which one we'll eat. Do you like Milky Way or Hershey's chocolate better?"

"Oh, you know that! My favorite is Hershey's!"

"Okay," Jarod said, reaching for the brown wrapper. "Then Hershey's it is."

"But wait," Jennifer put her hand on his arm. "If that one gets frozen solid, we can still break it and eat it. I even freeze them at home sometimes. But if the Milky Way gets real frozen, I don't know if we can eat it at all. So...I think we should eat the Milky Way right now."

Jarod smiled. "I never knew my little sister was such a food expert."

Jennifer giggled, "Well, only on candy and good stuff like that. I'm not so great on veggies."

"Me either!" Jarod said. "Even though Mom is always sticking cauliflower on my plate. I can't figure out why she likes that stuff."

"I don't know either," Jennifer said. "It's not even pretty to look at. I don't like broccoli very much either, but at least it kind of looks like trees, don't you think?"

"I don't know. I never really think about what my food looks like, just how it tastes." Jarod picked up the Milky Way. "And I'll bet this is going to taste really good." As he tried to split it, he realized that it was already partly frozen and was not going to be easy to break into two halves. "Jennifer, how about if we draw a line on it in the middle, and we'll each take bites until we get there."

Once again using his teeth, he tore the wrapper from the candy bar and then took a bite. "Hold out your hand," he said with a mouthful of caramel and chocolate. He put the candy bar in her hand and then held the flashlight as she took a bite. A look of pure joy crossed her face.

Jarod had to smile. "Hey, after we get home, we should write to Milky Way. They could do an ad on television about two kids stranded in a snow cave who were eating a Milky Way and make them look just the way you looked when you took that bite. They'd sell about a gazillion candy bars!"

"Uh-huh," Jennifer replied, the gooey, sweet candy sticking to her teeth. "Maybe we could even get to play the kids and they'd give us all the candy we ever wanted! We could each fill up our whole rooms with candy!"

"You can have the candy. I want money. I've got to get a new snowboard!"

Jennifer giggled, and she thought it felt so good to laugh. For a minute, she could almost pretend that they were some-where else. "Maybe you could get a snowboard made out of Milky Ways!"

"That'd be great until the sun came out. Then—good-bye, snowboard; hello, Milky Way mess!"

A tremble of cold went through Jennifer's body. "I'd settle for a little sun right now. I wonder what time it is?"

"The time? Hey—I don't know why I didn't think about it sooner. I have my watch on. Maybe it's already like almost midnight or something." Jarod forced himself to push the sleeves of his shell, his sweater, his turtleneck, and his long underwear up enough to see his watch. He was grateful for every piece of the layering he had. He took the flashlight and shined it directly on the face of the watch. "It's..." He looked more closely. "It says it's five o'clock."

"Five o'clock," Jennifer repeated sounding confused. "How can it be five o'clock when it's been dark for such a long time?"

Jarod sighed. "It must have been about that time when I got caught in the snowslide. My watch is broken." He tried to tell himself that it didn't matter. Until a few minutes ago, he'd forgotten that he was even wearing a watch. But that didn't make him feel any better. Now that he knew he had been wearing a watch, he wanted to be able to mark off the passing hours during the night.

He felt his own body shudder. His snowboard, his watch.... He wondered what else was broken or, worse yet, still going to break.

"Hey," Jennifer said, feeling his trembles, "your watch doesn't matter." She tried to think of something that would make him feel better. "Besides, Dad always says that watching the clock doesn't make the time go any faster. Right? So forget about your broken watch. If we're done eating, let's put the muffler on, and...um...um...we could play a game!"

"Play a game?" Jarod questioned. "Play a game!" he repeated, looking down at his broken watch and sounding close to crying.

Jennifer wished she had never brought up the whole thing about the time. She wished she hadn't made him feel so bad about his watch. She said, "Hey, you're probably afraid that you can't beat me even though you're my big brother."

Jarod shook his head. He sounded defeated. "I can't believe you're thinking about playing games when we're stuck out here like this!"

Jennifer reached across her body and patted his leg with her mittened hand. "Hey, Jarod...why not? Come on."

Jarod shrugged. He picked up the pink muffler, put it behind both of their necks, and wrapped it around the front of their necks up over their chins. His sister's face was right next to his. He felt like half of a pair of Siamese twins or at least what he thought one must feel like. He sighed deeply. "All right, Jen. Muffler on. What game do you want to play?"

"Let's play 'I'm thinking of something.' You get twenty guesses."

Jarod started to shake his head but realized that the muffler had bound it to Jennifer's too tightly for him to move his head at all. "Jen," he said. "Usually, when we play that, we think of something in the room. There's nothing here but snow and you and me, so that's not going to work very well, is it?"

"Well, fine, be that way," she said. "Then you think of a game!"

Jarod looked around their cave. Suddenly, it felt like a white prison.

Jennifer said again, "Come on, what game do you want to play?"

In frustration, Jarod answered, "Let's try the stay warm game!"

"The stay warm game?" Jennifer asked. "How about a nice warm bed with my electric blanket turned up to high." She sighed. "I wonder if..."

Jarod cut her off. He said. "No, a stay warm game right here."

"Okay," Jennifer said softly. "How do we play that?"

Jarod wanted to say that he didn't know. He wanted to say that there was no way to stay warm here. Then he heard Jennifer say, "Jarod, you aren't going to give up on us, are you?"

The panic he heard in her voice made him feel ashamed. He was the older one. He had to keep trying. "Course not." he said, trying to make his voice confident. "Hey, we never used that other sock. We're going to try your idea. In fact, you know how you're always saying Mom got your mittens two sizes too big. Well, let's see how big they are." Jarod put his gloved hand next to her mitten. It would be a tight squeeze, but he thought they almost could make it. He pulled his own glove off his left hand and told her to pull off her mitten on her right hand. "Oh! That's so cold!" she said.

"Hold my hand," Jarod ordered. He took the one unused sock and put both their hands into it, then wrapped the plastic around the sock. Using his teeth and his other hand, he pulled furiously to get her mitten back on both their hands. In holding Jennifer's hand, Jarod felt as if he were holding a block of ice.

"Now put your other hand in your pocket of your jacket. We should use every little extra layer we can."

"Okay." Jennifer carefully put the flashlight down on her lap, the light shining outward, and then put her hand in her pocket. Suddenly, the flashlight flickered, and there was blackness. Jennifer screamed. "No! It can't be dark in here all night Not that, too!"

CHAPTER 10

Jarod took his hand out of his pocket, felt for the flashlight, picked it up, and tapped it against his knee. The light shone brightly again. "Hey, Jen, it's okay. See, the light is still bright." But he worried about how long it would stay that way. He had no idea if his mom had put new batteries in, or if the flashlight really had been sitting in that backpack since the camping trip last summer. He could only hope it was like the TV commercial where the batteries kept going and going and going.

Jennifer squeezed his hand. "I'm sorry. I didn't mean to be such a baby. If it gets dark, I'll..." Her voice wavered. Then she continued, "I'll just know it will be light again in the morning."

Jarod squeezed her hand back and thought that her hand didn't feel quite so cold anymore. He felt that it was up to him to keep them both believing that they would get out of here and be safe. He said, "You know, we did a good job of tunneling back here to make this cave. Somehow, I think we almost went up at an angle, so the opening is down below us. With the backpack down there and us being up higher, it kind of keeps it not as cold, huh?"

Jennifer thought that it was still plenty freezing enough, but she could play the game, too. So she tried to make her voice sound happy as she said, "Yeah, and sitting on the snowboards was a good idea, too. It keeps us off the snow, and, you know, I think those mylar blanket things are working."

Jennifer giggled. "Wouldn't Mom be happy to see us sitting right next to each other and not even fighting?"

Jarod smiled back. It wasn't as if they had much choice about the closeness. The snow cave was only big enough for the two of them to sit side by side if they sat so that their shoulders, arms, and legs were touching. The entryway was really narrow and the ceiling was only a few inches taller than their heads. It was amazing that they'd ever actually gotten in here. Jarod figured that they'd have to dig the opening bigger to get out tomorrow morning, that was...if they made it through the night.

Jarod shook his head. He couldn't let himself think that way. But it was hard to stop his thoughts. They couldn't eat again for awhile. There were no more clothes or things in the backpack to use for warmth. There was nothing to do but just sit. It was so quiet—not just no television-quiet, but no birds, no animals, no noise of any kind. He wondered if it sounded like this when you were dead. His body trembled. "I have got to stop thinking this way!" he told himself. "How can we stay alive if I keep thinking about dead?"

Whether Jennifer felt his thoughts or was just uneasy about the silence herself, Jarod didn't know, but she said, "Maybe if we can't think of a game to play, we should at least tell stories or something."

"Okay, you start."

Jen shrugged. "I can't think of any. I was reading a book about this horse before we left for our ski trip, but it wasn't very good. Didn't you say that you guys all told stories around the campfire when you went camping last summer?"

"Yeah...but I don't exactly remember all of them."

"Okay. Just remember one of them."

"Well," Jarod answered. "Okay...I sort of remember this one about a guy who came to play basketball."

"Yeah," Jennifer said, "so what happened?"

"Well, it went like this. There were these two brothers. They were on a vacation, and they went to play basketball in a park not too far from their hotel. They brought a ball, and they hoped that when they got there, they could find a third person to make up a three-man team. Just as they were walking into the park, they saw a guy about their age walking toward them. The guy came up to them and asked them if they needed a third man for b-ball.

"The guys—their names were Gary and Andrew—said that an extra player would be great. His name was..." Jarod thought for a second. "His name was Matt. Anyway, he joined the other two and the three of them went over to the courts. Right before they started to play, Matt took his jacket off and laid it next to the basketball court. He told Andrew and Gary to remind him to take the coat home because it was brand new and his mom would really be mad if he lost it. Then they all started to play ball together. They made a really good team. Matt was a great shooter, but he knew when to pass, and he was never a ball hog. Team after team lined up on the sides to play, and each time, Matt, Andrew, and Gary won. Finally, after they had beaten five other teams, the game stopped, and other guys around the court began to clap. For the first time Matt looked down at his watch. 'Oh, no! I can't believe it's so late! It was great playing with you guys, but I've got to get home.' With that he waved and jogged off the court."

"But his jacket!" Jennifer said.

"I'm getting to that," Jarod replied.

"So Andrew and Gary hung around a little longer, but it wasn't much fun playing without Matt. As they started to gather the stuff they'd left on the sidelines, they looked down and saw Matt's letter jacket.

"Andrew said, 'Gee, I hate for this to get lost. Matt was such a nice guy. Too bad we don't know where he lives.'

"Gary looked at the inside of the letter jacket. It had a little label with Matt's name and address. 'I think this is only a few blocks from the hotel. Let's run it over to him.'

"So the two boys took the letter jacket and went to Matt's house. They rang the doorbell, and when a woman answered, they said, 'Hi, is Matt around?'

"The woman stared at the two boys, but she didn't look happy with them. 'Who are you,' she asked angrily, 'and what exactly is it that you want? You tell me right now, or I'm going to call the police!'

"Confused, the two boys took the letter jacket from behind their backs. 'We were playing ball with Matt, and we just wanted to return his jacket.'

"The woman gasped. 'That's impossible! That's not Matt's jacket!'

"So Andrew opened it to show the inside label, 'But it's got his name right here!'

"The mother grabbed the jacket. 'Where did you get this?'

she shouted at them. And then without waiting for an answer, she yelled, 'You tell me right now!'

"Gary looked at the mother and he said, 'Me and Matt and Andrew were just playing ball in the park a few blocks from here. Matt left his jacket at the end of the game. We were just trying to be nice and return it.'

"'The truth,' the woman said, shaking her finger at the boys. 'You tell me the truth this instant!'

"'But that is the truth!' Gary said. 'Look, if you don't believe us, just ask Matt. Isn't he here anyway?' There was silence. 'Hasn't Matt come home yet?' Gary asked."

Now Jarod started talking in a deep voice for effect. "The woman's cold, black eyes stared into Gary's. 'He isn't coming home," she said in a flat tone. 'Matt went to the park one day to play basketball. He was wearing this jacket coming home from the park when he was hit and killed by a drunk driver.' She took a deep breath—her cold eyes still staring at Andrew and Gary. 'Ten years ago today, we buried Matthew in this very jacket.'"

The flashlight flickered on the snow-covered walls. "Maybe telling stories isn't such a great idea after all," Jennifer said. The two sat in silence, and that seemed almost worse as both had their minds filled with thoughts of the dead basketball player.

Finally, Jennifer broke the silence. "Let's tell jokes instead. I've got one. Why does a chicken lay eggs?"

"I have no idea," Jarod replied.

" 'Cause they'd break if the chicken threw them. Get it?"

Jarod groaned, and Jennifer said, "Okay, see if you can do better."

"That won't be hard. Why did the turkey cross the road?"

"Uhh, to get to the other side?" Jennifer answered.

"Nope, to prove he wasn't chicken. Get it?"

"Okay," Jen said. "I've got one. What did the digital clock say to its mother?"

"Uh, time for a change?"

"Nope," Jennifer said. "Look, Ma! No hands."

"Why's a dog hot in summer?" Jarod asked.

"I don't know."

"Because it's got a coat and pants! Get it?"

"My turn," Jennifer said. "Why doesn't an ocean ever say hello? Because it just waves instead!"

"Yeah? Well, do your feet smell? Does your nose run? Then you're built upside down!" Jarod said.

"Okay, here's one. What did one firecracker say to the other?" Jennifer asked.

"Happy Fourth of July?" Jarod answered.

"Nope. My pop's bigger than your pop," Jennifer giggled.

"Yeah? Well, do you know what time it is when an elephant sits on your fence?"

"Time to get a new fence!" Jennifer shouted triumphantly. "I know that one!"

The jokes got stupider and stupider, and they knew it, but they told them with even greater speed, hoping that somehow the humor could cover the fear they felt from the night and the cold and the cave. And for every joke Jarod remembered, Jennifer knew three.

Jarod sighed. "I don't know, Jen. Maybe you're going to be a professional joke teller when you grow up. I can't believe you know so many."

Jennifer coughed. "Oh...I'm not so great. For lots of the days when everyone else got to go outside for recess, I had to stay in because of my breathing. I spent most of that time in the library reading joke books. I tried to find things to laugh about because I felt so bad about not getting to go out and play with everyone."

Jarod frowned. He hadn't even thought of Jennifer's breathing since they'd been in the snow cave. "So how are you doing right now?"

Jennifer coughed again. "Okay. I'm doing okay. Pretty soon, I may take another spray." She tried to think about the way she really felt. Her chest had hurt and felt tight ever since she had been resting right before the snowslide. Still, she wasn't really wheezing, and that was good. She knew it would help a lot if she could just get warm.

"Jarod, do you really think that there are people out there looking for us?"

Jarod had been wondering the same thing himself. "Sure," he said. "There are probably airplanes and guys on skis and maybe even tracking dogs, like in that movie we saw on TV."

"But how will they ever see us buried here in the snow?"

Jarod squeezed his sister's hand. "Hey, remember, we've got your skis standing up and crossed in the distress sign. They'll see them. And when they get close to us, we'll hear them, and we'll start shouting back, and then we'll come out of here, and we'll be rescued."

She tapped her mitten against her leg. "That sounds so good. I wish they would come right now!"

Jarod wished so, too. "Well, you can be sure that if we were supposed to meet Mom and Dad at 4:15, Mom had already contacted the ski patrol by 4:30. So it isn't like they didn't know we were lost right away."

Jennifer still worried. She was pretty sure her brother was right about the two of them having been reported lost. Her mother had been worried enough about letting her ski. Jennifer felt terrible thinking about how scared her mother must be now. "Maybe that Eric guy saw us go off the ski slope, and when they put it on the news and stuff that we were lost, maybe he told the police that he saw us, and so the police already know where to look."

"Probably so," Jarod said. "Even if Eric didn't see us, there were lots of people on the slope." Actually, he didn't think anyone had been paying any attention to them, except maybe Eric, and that jerk certainly wasn't going to help them, but Jarod didn't say anything about his true thoughts.

"Maybe we could have a little more chicken soup," Jennifer said.

Jarod unscrewed the lid, and they each took another couple of sips, again swirling the warm liquid in their mouths each time to make it last. Yet even so, the warmth seemed to disappear in an instant. "Could we have just a little more?" Jennifer pleaded.

Jarod took the flashlight and shined it into the thermos. They'd already had more than half of the contents. He thought they should wait a little longer for more or it would never last the night. Then his eye caught sight of a foil wrapper. "I think we should save the soup, but I've got something else to keep us warm," he told his sister.

Jarod leaned down and unwrapped the foil of one of their four handwarmers. He bent it as the directions said and told Jennifer, "Let's try this in the glove we're sharing. That way, both of us can get warm, only using one handwarmer." It wasn't easy trying to get the mitten off their hands, but they finally did it, and Jarod slipped the handwarmer inside the sock, between their two hands. In a couple of minutes, both could feel the warmth begin to flow into their numb fingers.

"Oh, this feels so good," Jennifer said. "I wish I had one for my whole body."

Jarod agreed, and while he was wishing, he wished he knew how much longer it was until morning. It seemed like they had been in here forever.

Neither one of them could think of anything more to talk about, so they were silent. After a while, Jarod heard a noise break the silence. His heart began to pound. It was the first noise of any kind he had heard since they'd entered the snow cave. It sounded so close. Then he realized that it was Jennifer's soft snoring. She had fallen asleep. In a way, he envied her, for the time would pass much faster than just sitting here awake like he was.

Jarod wondered if the flashlight were growing dimmer, or if it was just that his eyes hurt from the cold. He felt himself yawn and then tried to shake his head, but the muffler kept it from moving much. He knew he had to stay awake because he remembered hearing on the news about homeless people who had fallen asleep on cold nights and frozen to death. He bit his lip as a picture of rescuers finding their frozen bodies in this cave suddenly filled his mind. He forced the thought away. He would stay awake and keep an eye on Jennifer, too. He would because he had to, but what could he think of to keep his brain going? Jarod's mind was an absolute blank. It seemed to him that there was nothing in his life but this white frozen prison. He couldn't help himself. He yawned again. His head felt a little fuzzy, and he told himself that maybe he could just sleep for a few minutes. If he didn't stay asleep for very long, it might even help him think better.

CHAPTER 11

Minutes, or maybe it was hours later, Jarod forced his unwilling eyes to open. He wanted more than anything to go back to sleep. He didn't feel cold when he was asleep. He didn't have to try to figure out what to do when he was asleep. But a part of his brain kept prodding him awake. Part of his mind knew how dangerous it was to stay asleep. His body felt so stiff and so cold. It almost didn't feel as if it belonged to him. He knew he had to do something to stay awake or he would fall asleep again. "Eat!" he said aloud. "We should eat something else."

He went to reach for another granola bar, but his hand and arm didn't move. He looked at his arm almost as if it didn't belong to him. "I will not let this happen," he told himself. "I can still move my hands and feet." He stared at his arm. Almost as if it was another person, he told it sternly, "Move, arm!" Slowly, painfully, he felt himself move his arm and hand. Then he turned his attention to his sister. She had been sleeping much longer than he had. "Jen," he said softly. There was no answer. "Jennifer!" he called loudly. Still no answer. He nudged her hard with his elbow, and yelled again, "Jennifer, wake up!"

He could feel her body begin to stir next to him. "Ohhhhh," she sort of groaned.

"Don't go back to sleep," he commanded. "Listen to me. Don't sleep. Talk to me."

"I...I'm very tired. Talk later," came her foggy voice.

"No!" Jarod screamed, feeling suddenly more awake as his heart pounded. "Talk to me now, Jen. You can't fade away. Wake up!" He nudged her hard with his elbow.

"Ouch!" she cried.

"Good," he said. "It's good that you feel that!"

His fear and adrenaline had kicked in, and he could feel himself much more alert. He unscrewed the lid to the chicken soup and put the warm thermos to her nose. "Smell this. Come on, you can have a sip of it, but you've got to wake up." He squeezed her hand tightly inside the mitten.

It seemed to Jarod that he kept shouting and nudging Jennifer forever, and she kept falling back asleep, but finally, she seemed to stay awake. "Why couldn't you just let me sleep!" she sighed. "I feel so awful."

"No," he shouted again. "If we sleep, we'll die. We have to eat. We have to move. We are going to live!"

"Uh-huh," Jennifer said, still foggy.

Jarod lifted the thermos to her mouth. "Wake up enough to take a sip because we don't have enough to waste a single drop!" He held the thermos near Jennifer for a couple of minutes. His hand tingled so much that he worried he would drop the container and its precious contents. Finally, Jennifer took a couple of sips of the liquid and shuddered. He took a couple of sips himself and then quickly replaced the lid.

"Okay," he said as much to himself as to her. "Now, we'll each have another granola bar, and then we'll do...we'll do something."

He had stuck the remaining granola bars inside his jacket between his sweater and his turtleneck in an effort to keep them from freezing. Getting to the granola bars meant having to unzip his jacket, and Jarod struggled to make it happen. Finally, he reached into his sweater and pulled out another granola bar. He tore at it to open it, took a bite, then placed it in Jennifer's mouth and told her to take a bite. She did as she was told, but he felt almost as if he were dealing with a robot. Still, he continued taking a bite of the granola bar and putting it in her mouth for her to take a bite as well. By the time they had finished the simple task of eating the snack, Jarod was exhausted and worried. How could they get down to the bottom of the slope if just eating a simple granola bar had worn him out so totally? Jarod tried to think. What else could they do?

"We've got to keep moving," he said. Then he thought, Yeah, right. How can we move? We're wedged in this thing so tightly. He turned off the flashlight, peered down to the opening, and hoped he would see light streaking in from outside, but it was totally dark. Not morning yet, he thought. We can't leave this place yet, and we can't just sit here. So what could they do? Jarod kept trying to think. His legs felt like pieces of wood. He managed to make himself lift one a little and then the other. Then it hit him. That was it—they could exercise. Even if they couldn't get up and go outside, they could still move around a little bit.

"Jennifer, lift up your right leg. Look at mine. Lift up your right leg."

"I don't want to. It's too hard."

Suddenly, he had an idea. "Hey, Jen. Remember the song Mom used to do with us when we were little kids. Come on. We're going to do it now."

"Oh, is Mommy here?" Jennifer asked.

Jarod tried to fight his own panic. "Not right now," he answered, "but we're going to do this little song for her. Ready?" He began singing, "Head, shoulders, knees, and toes," and moving his hands to each of the spots as he sang them. He grasped her right hand tighter in the mitten they shared and pulled her arm and hand with his as he touched each area.

He repeated it over and over. Finally, Jennifer picked up her other arm and began to repeat the gestures with him. Soon they were singing the song they had learned as babies and doing the accompanying gestures.

"Good job, Jen! Good job!" Jarod said, and he meant it. Jennifer seemed more alert now, and it felt so good to have her back. He started to say, "I thought you were going to..." and then he stopped himself and said, "sleep while I did all the work."

"Moving around kind of helps the cold, huh, Jarod?" Jennifer asked.

"Yeah, I think it does." They tried lifting their legs a little, then their arms. They turned their heads from side to side in unison so that they didn't have to take off the muffler. They tried raising their shoulders up, then down a hundred times, and then they started all over again.

"Let's put our hands on the snowboards and see if we can lift our butts off it." Jarod said. "Maybe if we can lift them up and let our butts hit the board, we can get some feeling back into them." They tried, but it was impossible to use the hand they had put into one mitten, so Jarod found his own stiff-fingered glove and forced it on his hand. Their arms were so weak that it was hard for them to lift their bodies, but they forced themselves to try. At first, their backsides were so cold that neither of them felt anything when they hit the board each time, but after about ten times, they could each begin to feel a stinging sensation. Jarod insisted that they start over again at the very beginning of the exercises, and he began singing the silly baby song again and gesturing with it. Jennifer followed. Jarod thought that maybe it had even begun to feel a little warmer. "We just have to keep thinking," he reminded himself. "The exercise is going to work. We can beat this!" He would not let them go to sleep again. He would not let them sit and think about all the awful things that could happen. They would just keep moving, and soon it would be morning. Then they would crawl out of this cave, and they would get home!

He began to push himself and Jennifer to exercise even harder. When they got to the part about raising themselves with their arms, Jennifer gasped, "I can't, Jarod..." There were ragged, gasping wheezes, and then, "I just can't do this any more... I can't breathe."

CHAPTER 12

Jarod grabbed Jennifer's jacket pocket and pulled her inhaler from it. He shoved it into her mittened hand, and she lifted it to her lips and took a deep spray. Jarod took a deep breath with her, almost as if that should somehow help. She sucked the medication in, then breathed out slowly, allowing the medication to fill her lungs. Still, the next breath she took was ragged and wheezing. She shook her inhaler, put it to her lips, and pushed on it to release more medication. Once again pausing, then breathing out slowly, she waited for the medication to give her some relief. Her chest hurt, and she tried to fight the panic she felt when her breathing got like this. "Relax," the doctor had told her over and over again. "You can help control your breathing. Don't panic. Try to breathe evenly. Practice the exercises you've learned." She tried to do everything he had said. There could be no emergency room tonight. She would have to do it all herself. "I can do it!" she said aloud.

"Huh?" Jarod said. "Jen, are you okay? Can I do something?"

Jennifer could feel the pressure on her chest begin to let up a little. "I'm going to be all right," she replied, feeling relief that this wasn't going to be one of the really bad episodes. The medication was working. She focused on her breathing just the way her doctor had said to and tried to make her body relax.

Within a few minutes, she could tell that the wheezing had gotten much better.

"Hey, I'm sorry," Jarod said when he could hear her breathing normally again. "I guess I pushed too hard on the exercise stuff. I feel like a jerk."

"Ah, Jarod. Don't. You know that stuff that is normal for other people can set my asthma off. Half the time I don't know what's going to start it. Sometimes, everything is fine, and sometimes, dumb little stuff makes it so I can't breathe at all. I guess that's why Mom gets so worried about me." Jennifer drew her arm across her face, and Jarod didn't really want to look because he thought she might be crying again. Then she said, "I was thinking that this whole thing is so...I don't know, so crazy. If Mom hadn't been so worried about me, she would have let you go with your friends. Then you probably would have never run into Eric, and we'd all be back safe and warm at the hotel."

Jarod tried to put on a brave front. "Yeah, but by tomorrow night we *will* be back at the hotel with Mom and Dad, and once I'm there, I may never come out of a hot shower. They may have to just put a sign on the door that says the room is permanently occupied!" He closed his eyes and tried to imagine the hot water pounding on his body. Just the thought of it made him feel a little warmer. "Let's think of all the things that make us really warm," he said.

"I don't know," Jennifer said. "It's pretty hard to think warm anything right now."

"Try," Jarod urged.

Jennifer thought. "I know. How about when I went to your

Little League baseball game last summer. You know, the one where it was in the afternoon, and it was so hot that Jimmy Frederick's grandmother fainted."

"Yeah," Jarod remembered. "And I was so hot after I hit that home run that I practically puked." He tried to make his body remember what a little of that heat might be like, and then he said, "Hey, and how about that time in the summer when we went to the mall for the whole morning, and when we came out and got into the car, I burned my hand on the door handle."

"Yeah," Jennifer said. "In Arizona, the car after it sits out in the summer is about the hottest place of all. It's funny. I can remember being really hot, my face getting red and stuff, but right now, I can't make myself feel what that felt like." She sighed. "I wonder how long we've been here. When we're sleeping, the night seems to go so much faster."

Jarod couldn't argue with that, but he knew that they had to stay awake. They had to keep talking, so they did. "Do you like going to Miller Elementary better than Steck?" Jennifer asked.

Jarod shrugged. "Not really. Do you?"

Jennifer didn't answer. "How come you liked Steck better?"

"I dunno. I guess I started school at Steck, so I knew it better." Jarod thought for a minute. "Maybe that wasn't it. It was just that at Steck, I was always really popular. But after we moved and I started Miller, I was just another kid." Jarod thought again. "I don't know why. Everything changed. It's weird, but when Jeff asked me to go snowboarding with him and his friends, that was the first time I ever got really included with the popular kids here. And I figured that my snowboarding was good enough that they'd think I was okay. "

Jennifer sighed. "And then because of me, you didn't get to go."

Jarod shrugged. "That doesn't really matter now. Know something? In a way, when we first went out of bounds, I thought it was so cool. I thought maybe I'd go back to school and I'd have these great stories to tell about being the first one to carve my own slope."

"Well," Jennifer said, "after we get rescued, you can still tell them that you made your own slope and that you survived an avalanche, too. That will be exciting enough for anyone to stop and listen. None of those other guys will have anything as good."

"You know, Jen, you're okay. Thanks. And what about you? Which school do you like better?" he asked.

Jennifer didn't answer.

"Come on. I told you how I felt," Jarod said.

"Okay, I guess I like it here a lot better. I had to stay in from recess a lot in Denver, and it seemed like I never got to go to P.E. Other kids either felt sorry for me or thought I was weird. And that school nurse there—she was more scared of my asthma than I was. But here, at Miller, it's been okay. I mean, there are some bad days, but most of them are okay."

Jarod considered what his sister's life at school in Denver must have been like. It was weird. Though the two of them had always gone to school together, Jarod had never really thought about his sister's life before.

In that cold cave, sitting so close to each other, both continued to talk. They shared what they liked or didn't like at school, what they wanted to do when they grew up, what they liked or didn't like about their friends, and times when they had been embarrassed or felt left out. Jarod had never said most of these things to anyone, and he certainly had never talked to his sister like this before. Finally, after sharing things they'd never planned to tell anyone, they had both run out of things to say. The flashlight flickered dimly, and their bodies cast strange shadows on the snow. Still, morning had not come.

Jennifer said, "I think we better exercise a little again. I feel like everything is getting frozen stiff." This time, Jarod let her set the pace. They both moved pretty slowly, but at least they could still move their bodies. Jarod looked at the other three handwarmers. He had hoped to save them to use on their way down the slope in the morning, but he was so cold. He broke open another one of them, and lifting his hat just a tiny bit on the left side, he placed the handwarmer between his and Jennifer's cheeks and ears. They had to sit still to hold the warmer between them like that, and it took a number of minutes before Jarod even began to feel his face thaw. His ear burned from the heat, though the warmer itself wasn't that hot.

Jennifer moaned softly. "Oh, I wish I could have a giant one of these all over."

Unfortunately, the last of the packet's warmth faded away too soon, and Jarod moved his head away enough to let the packet drop. He pulled his hat down over the warmed spot.

Jennifer took her mittened hand from her pocket and shook it in the air. "I have to look at it to keep knowing that it's there."

Jarod knew what she meant. His own hand was freezing, too. Then he got an idea. He didn't know why he hadn't thought of it earlier. If the granola bar and the candy had stayed warmer because they were inside his clothes, why didn't he do the same thing with his hands? He explained his plan to Jennifer; then they both undid their jackets enough to slide their arms from the sleeves and fold them across their chests. It was no easy task to get the jackets zipped again, but helping each other, and using their teeth, they managed. Their hands were tucked in their underarms. It wasn't the most comfortable way to sit, but it did seem to help.

"Let's sing," Jennifer said into the silence.

"Sing what?" Jarod asked.

"I don't know, but I'm getting real tired again. And the last time, when you woke me, I could barely wake up. What if the next time..."

Jarod didn't want her to think about that, so he cut in. "Okay, so we'll sing. We can do 'Ninety-nine Bottles of Beer on the Wall.' By the time we finish, it will have to be morning."

"Well..."

"Well, what?" Jarod said. "Don't tell me you don't know the words!"

"I know them. I'm not dumb. It's just that...well...I don't think we're supposed to sing about beer."

In spite of how bleak everything looked, Jarod started laughing. "Jennifer, in case you forgot, we're stuck here in a cave made out of snow. We're lost, there's no sign of any other human being, and it's the middle of the night? I don't believe you!"

And so they sang. By the time they were down to ten bottles of beer, their voices were getting hoarse. When they got to three bottles of beer, Jarod forced his hands out of the jacket, picked up the flashlight, and turned off its light. "Hey," Jennifer started to scream, and then she stopped—for the first rays of morning sunlight were peeking through the cave's entrance.

Jennifer began to wiggle around where she sat and in a hushed, awe-filled voice said, "We did it, Jarod! We made it through the night here. Now we can go home." She began to cry softly. "I didn't think I'd ever really see Mommy and Daddy again. I didn't think we'd ever really get out of this cave."

Jarod stared at the entrance, his eyes feasting on the half-light that had begun to filter in. "Oh, please," he prayed, "when we crawl out of here, let us see that we are almost to the bottom. Let someone see us and help us."

He felt Jennifer nudging him. "Can we go?"

"Let's think before we start. We need to figure out how we are going to do everything. First, I think we should eat the other granola bar and finish the chicken soup so we have energy to get to the bottom."

"And the handwarmers, don't forget those, " Jennifer said.

"Right. We'll take those with us and use them wherever we feel the worst when we get out of here. We'll put the mylar blankets back in the backpack and take them with us. Anything else?"

Jennifer shook her head no, and the two of them forced themselves to finish the food they'd planned. All night they'd thought about eating these things, and now that they could,

90

they just wanted to hurry. They knew they needed the strength the food would give, but it was hard to think about food when freedom seemed so close. They worked to get the mylar blankets from underneath them and behind them. Jarod's hands were too cold to try to fold the mylar carefully. He just squashed each blanket into a small ball, reached for the backpack, and shoved them into it. Next he stuffed the handwarmers and flashlight into the bag. Then, he pulled the snowboard from underneath him and began to dig away more snow to make it easier to get out of the cave. The snow had hardened and was not easy to budge. "Okay," he said. "I'll go out first and check it out. Then you'll come, and we'll be on our way home!"

Jarod slid on his back down toward the opening. Using the bottoms of his feet, he kicked at the opening to make it larger, pushed the backpack through it, and then slid through himself. Once outside, he blinked his to see the sunrise. The sky was just beginning to be streaked with yellow and gold light.

"Hey," Jennifer called, "is it okay if I come now?"

Jarod had not yet tried to stand up. He simply slid a little further out of the way of the cave's entrance. "Make sure you have your inhalers and come on."

In a minute, Jennifer was sitting next to him in the snow outside their cave's entrance. Her body shook. It seemed impossible, but it had been warmer being surrounded by snow in the cave at night than it was out here this morning. Jennifer cupped her hands over her eyes, as did Jarod, and both looked to where they thought they should see the bottom of the mountain. But there seemed to be no bottom, only endless white snow.

CHAPTER 13

"**T**he bottom has to be close!" Jarod fumed. "We aren't giving up now!" He stayed angry so he wouldn't cry. "Let's get your skis so we can get going!"

Jennifer sounded defeated. "Where are we going? We don't even know."

"Yes! We do. We're going to the bottom. We must just not be as far down as we thought we were."

Suddenly, Jennifer felt afraid to leave the cave. At least they had been safe there. "Maybe we should stay here, and we can let the dogs and the rescuers find us here."

Jarod was too cold and too weary to argue. Besides, what was the point of telling her that this was a huge mountain and it might be days before dogs or rescuers found them. He forced himself to stand up. His legs felt very rubbery, but he was determined not to let them give out under him. His feet, he didn't feel at all. Grabbing Jennifer's skis, he put them down in the snow and ordered her to put them on right away.

"But..." Jennifer sniffled, still sitting in the snow. "Those skis were our sign. How will airplanes see us now?"

Jarod looked at his terrified sister. "Jen, don't freak out now. We've come this far. The rescuers don't need to see the skis any more. If they're looking for us, it's daytime, and it's sunny, and they will see us. Now come on, put the skis on and let's get going."

Jennifer didn't say anything. She struggled to get her skis on, struggled to get up, and then promptly fell down again into the snow. "I'm so tired, Jarod. Maybe you could just take my skis and go get help."

"Jennifer, you're not making sense. Your skis won't fit me. Come on. You're just scared. If you just get going, we can be in the warm ski lodge with the fire going real soon."

Jennifer nodded and wobblingly stood again. Her legs were so unsure that she was afraid to ski down the mountain, so she skied across it instead. Jarod called to her, "Jen, that won't take us anywhere. Turn and come back this way, and then let's head down."

Jennifer fell again as she tried to turn, and she lay in the snow. It was hopeless, but Jarod kept yelling and encouraging and pleading, and so she forced herself to get up once again. She came back toward her brother, and her legs began to feel a little sturdier.

When she got close to him, Jennifer noticed that Jarod was holding one piece of the broken blue snowboard. "What are you going to do with that?" Jennifer asked.

"Use it as a sled," Jarod said. He put the board under himself, then pulled his knees close to his chest to make room for his legs to fit. Reaching around his bent legs, he grasped onto the jagged front edge of the board. "Okay," he said. "Here I go." He pushed off to show Jennifer the way down. His snowboard-sled quickly picked up speed, then hit a bump. Jarod tried to hold onto the front, but he found himself tossed into the snow. He looked up from a face full of snow just in time to see the runaway board take off.

Jennifer made her way down to him. Jarod rolled over onto his back and forced himself to a sitting position. Trying to keep his voice from breaking, he said, "Jen, I'm going to need one of your poles. I'll have to try to walk down the slope."

It was hard work. The pure powder that had seemed so perfect when he'd had a snowboard to glide across it was impossible now. Jarod found himself sinking into the snow again and again. Each step grew harder. Jennifer waited for him a ways below, and he could see her body shiver as she stood on her skis. By the time he reached her, he was out of breath and feeling sweaty. This was just too hard. Without skis or snowshoes or something, he couldn't keep moving.

Jennifer looked at her brother. He looked awful. "I think we should rest here," she said.

"Got to keep going," he panted. "Can't stop." He knew he was too tired to walk any further, so he sat down. He would be a human sled. He would slide down on his butt. "Go," he told Jennifer. "Go now." He began to slide on his back, but some-how, his foot caught him, and he rolled over. Then he began rolling downward uncontrollably. He felt his belly and his face hit the snow, and then his back, and he threw his hands up to cover his face before he tumbled over on it again. Dimly, he heard Jennifer scream as he rolled and rolled and rolled.

Jennifer watched her brother, helpless to stop him, horrified to watch him turning into a human snowball. Finally, Jarod must have hit an even spot on the slope. He stopped rolling. "Get up," she cried. "Oh, Jarod, are you okay?" But there was no answer. It was like the snowslide all over again, but this time, the mountain hadn't moved, only Jarod, and this time, he was much weaker because of everything that had already happened to him. Jennifer put her skis together and hurried to reach him. After all that had happened, there was a kind of recklessness to her skiing. When she got to Jarod, he was lying face down in the snow. "Jarod," she kept screaming as she pulled off her skis and bent over him. "Jarod!" She shook him, and using all her strength, she turned him over on his back and began rubbing his face with the dry muffler he had insisted she wear.

His eyes fluttered open. "Hey, Jen," he croaked, and then he shut his eyes again.

Jennifer tried to shake him, and when that didn't work, she began rubbing his face again with the muffler and urging him to open his eyes. When he finally did, she said, "Jarod, you've got to get up now. We have to keep going! Come on, you can do it. You're a tough guy. You're my big brother."

Jarod's voice was thick. "It's okay, Jen. I'm not even cold any more. Why don't you take my jacket. Go on. Just take it. I'm just going to go to sleep for a little while here."

Jennifer screamed at him, but it was as if he didn't really hear her or care what she was saying. She didn't know what to do. She couldn't make him get up. She couldn't leave him, and they couldn't stay here. She looked at her brother. He had a strange kind of smile on his face. She had to do something. But what! How could a kid not even nine years old know what the right thing was!

She couldn't get him to stand up, and she knew she shouldn't just let him lie in the snow. Then she noticed that somehow, in spite of all the rolling, Jarod still had the back-pack on. She reached under him and pulled it first off one shoulder and then reached around the other side and pulled it off the other. Using her teeth as she had seen Jarod do, she pulled open the zipper to get to the mylar blankets. Pulling them out, she saw her goggles fall out from the spot she had put them last night. It was hard work, but she managed to get one of the blankets under most of Jarod's body by turning him a little at a time. Then she made the backpack into a ball and put it under Jarod's head like a pillow. Breaking open both the handwarmers, she put them under Jarod's hat, one by each ear. For a moment, she wanted to grab the handwarmers and hold on to them herself. "Jarod," she kept saying. "Please get up! Please. I can't be in charge. I don't know what I should do."

"No, it's nice here," Jarod said in a voice that didn't even sound like him. Jennifer suddenly knew that no matter what she said, her brother was not going to move. He wasn't being Jarod. He wasn't making any sense. She put the other blanket on top of Jarod. Its shiny surface gleamed in the sunlight so much that it hurt Jennifer's eyes. She grabbed her goggles and put them on while she tried to decide what to do next. Deep inside, she knew. It was crazy. Jarod was the brave one. Jarod was the great snowboarder, but somehow she was the one who was going to have to find the bottom of this mountain and get them help. Her chest hurt. She reached for her inhaler. This was all wrong. This was not the way to use an inhaler. The doctor had said too much of it was harmful. But what differ-ence did that make now, she asked herself. She and Jarod were going to die unless she did something. She took two more sprays of her inhaler. Then leaning over her brother, she kissed his forehead. "I'm going to get help for us, Jarod. You stay awake, and you keep thinking about that hot shower, you hear? You keep thinking that tonight, we're going to be at the hotel with Mommy and Daddy. Jarod, do you hear me?"

"Yeah," Jarod said, and Jennifer felt a little better. Then he added, "If I don't get to pitch, I don't want to play."

He was making no sense. Heart pounding, Jennifer walked back to her skis. Her feet were so numb that she couldn't even feel that her boots were in her bindings. She had to look at them to see. She squeezed her eyes shut for a minute and in a ragged voice, said, "Jarod, I love you," and then she forced herself to ski downward.

As she skied, she tried to tell herself that she could do this. She could and she would save both of them. She let herself stop for a minute and glanced back up the hill to the bright silver that was there. Part of her wished she had lain down next to Jarod and drifted off to sleep with him. She skied and she cried. The bottom of this mountain—where was it? How could they have gone this far and still not even seen it? Maybe this mountain had no bottom to it.

Jennifer's legs became shakier and shakier and her breathing more and more ragged. She wanted to stop, to rest for awhile, but she forced herself to keep going. She had promised Jarod that she would get them help. She was starting to feel kind of funny inside. Her eyes burned and her head began buzzing. Then she heard whistles in her head. She giggled. She could whistle with her mouth, too, not as loud as her head, but she could make her mouth answer her head's whistle. She stopped and leaned on her poles. Her lips were parched and cold, but she made them whistle any way. This was more fun than skiing. The whistle in her head got even louder, so she made her voice whistle louder, too. The noise continued. The next whistle was so loud that it almost sounded as if it were coming outside her head, but she wasn't fooled. She knew that no one in the whole world was here except her and Jarod, and even Jarod was back up the mountain.

Then she saw a man on a snowmobile. She thought she should tell him that this wasn't a very safe place to be, but she decided that he wasn't real anyway, so it didn't matter. Then the man on the snowmobile was right next to her. She giggled again. "Hello. You aren't real. I know that. I'm real. My brother is real, or at least we used to be real."

The imaginary man asked, "Where is your brother?" so Jennifer told him. She said that she had covered Jarod with a shiny blanket and he was going to take a little rest. Then Jennifer watched as the man took out a thing that looked like a telephone. She only vaguely heard him shout, "I've got the girl! Repeat! I've got the little girl! She's disoriented, but she says the brother is up the slope a ways from here." She heard him keep talking about coordinates on the slope and something about his GPS. Then he started talking about cats, and she giggled again. Silly, imaginary man. What good were cats on a mountain in the snow?

The silly man got a big jacket out of a bag on the snowmobile. He took her pretty pink one off of her and put the big jacket on. She felt him pull the wet mittens from her hands and put on others. She giggled again. "Silly man, silly man," she sang. "Plan, plan plan." She felt herself being lifted onto the snowmobile. It made noise, but it didn't go anywhere at all. And then her imagination got even better. This big tractor thing came rumbling up the snow, and the next thing she knew, she was in it. It felt like lots of blankets were on top of her, but she wasn't sure if it was really blankets or if the snow from the cave had just fallen in and covered her up. Maybe that was it. Maybe that was why she couldn't really move.

CHAPTER 14

Things were very confusing. Jennifer couldn't really move, but it felt like she was being bumped around. She was all by herself, but she could hear other people talking, and then the bumpiness stopped, and she got lifted up and put in something else.

Some man kept leaning over her and talking to her. She couldn't quite figure out what he was doing or where she was. She tried to ask him. At first, he didn't pay any attention. Finally, he said something about an ambulance, a paramedic, and some other stuff that was just too hard to hear. Just in case he was real at all, she tried to talk. "Brother? Jarod. Big brother. Fell down." She could feel that she was crying, "Rolled over and over. Help Jarod? Help Jarod!"

The voice seemed to understand. It said something about Jarod and another ambulance. Jennifer tried to make sure. "Help Jarod," she repeated.

The voice answered, "Jarod is getting help." Jennifer smiled. That was good. She began to sing softly, "One hundred bottles of beer on the wall." She could hear sirens. They seemed to sing with her.

Then the nice voice took her inside a place he said was a hospital, and that voice went away. There were lots of others, but they didn't make much sense. It was mostly noise. Then she heard one she knew really well. "My babies!" it cried. "Are my babies okay?"

"Mommy?" she called.

Then she heard another voice. She tried to stay awake, but it was so hard. Finally, she gave up.

When Jennifer opened her eyes again, everything looked foggy and white. So they were still in the snow. The rest had only been a dream. Or wait. Maybe they were in heaven. That was white, too. It didn't really matter. Wherever she was, at least she finally felt warm. Then she reached up to rub her eyes, but as she reached, something moved, and the white went away. Slowly, Jennifer realized that the white had only been her bed sheet in her eyes, and she was in a room.

There was a steel railing on her bed, but she could see through it and see that there was another bed in the room. This must be a hospital, she thought, and then she called, "Jarod? Jarod, is that you in that other bed?"

There was no answer. "Jarod!" she shouted louder, and in a moment, a nurse was walking into the room.

"Shh...it's all right," the nurse soothed.

"My brother...is he...he was there under the shiny blanket...I tried..."

The nurse interrupted. "Relax. Your brother is going to be okay. He's in the other bed. You did a good job of helping to keep him safe, but he was much colder than you were when you two were rescued. Your brother has had a rough time, and he's very tired now. Let's let him sleep."

"But is he okay?"

"He will be," the nurse reassured. "Your parents have been

waiting for you to wake up. They'll be back very soon. I'll let them know you're awake. Why don't you just rest until they come."

Jennifer's eyes filled with tears. She was really going to see her parents again. If only Jarod would wake up so he could see them, too.

CHAPTER 15

Later that day, the Golden family had quite a reunion. Mrs. Golden hugged the children and cried and cried. Mr. Golden kept going first to one bed and then the other to put an arm around each child.

Two days later, the children were waiting to be released from the hospital when a man walked into their room and removed his hat. "I'm Sergeant Nate Elkun. I was the head of the search and rescue operation that looked for you, and I don't mind telling you that the two of you gave us quite a scare."

Jarod looked guilty. "I am so sorry. I don't ever plan to go outside the marked boundaries again."

The Sergeant replied, "Well, that's good to know. I wouldn't want to make a habit of having to look for you. And more than forty folks from the ski patrol and the sheriff's department will be glad to hear it, too."

Jarod whistled, "Wow, all those people were looking for us?"

"Yes, they were. We had folks out on skis, snowshoes, and snowmobiles. We even had a helicopter out. Once we found your sister, we got her into the SnowCat and sent paramedics on snowmobiles up to start working on you. Then the SnowCat picked you up and took both of you to waiting ambulances. The ambulances brought you both here."

Sgt. Elkun continued. "We found your snow cave. You didn't do a half-bad job of building it. How did you know that making the entrance lower than you were sitting would help keep in the heat?"

"We didn't," Jennifer said. "It just kind of worked out that way when we dug."

Sgt. Elkun shook his head. "Well, that was lucky because it's a good survival technique. And speaking of survival tips, you should have stayed at the snow cave, left your skis crossed, and you definitely should have stayed together. We'd have found you faster and in better condition." He sighed, "Truth was, it was a real good thing we found you when we did. You, young man, were on the verge of severe hypothermia, and that's very serious stuff."

Jarod shivered for a minute in spite of the room's warmth. His mother spoke with a catch in her voice, "Sergeant Elkun, we're so very grateful to all of you. There are no words to say thanks for the many hours you and all your searchers spent in the cold and the dark looking for the children. We'll never forget any of you."

Sgt. Elkun looked at her and then fixed his gaze on the children. "We'll remember you, too." He nodded toward Jarod. "Maybe all the news about what happened to you will stop other people from crossing those boundary lines. I don't know when folks are going to realize that those markers are there for a good reason. Crossing them can be like playing with a loaded gun."

His parents thanked the officer again. Jarod reached out

104

and shook the man's hand. Thinking about the cold and the miserable night he'd caused for Sgt. Elkun and the other searchers, Jarod felt too bad to even look his rescuer in the eye as he said good-bye. The room grew quiet. Jarod shivered. He'd almost killed his sister and himself, all to show off in front of some dumb bully.

A woman with long dark hair in a white coat strode quickly into the room and broke the silence. She introduced herself as Dr. Lori Maulken, examined Jarod's left foot, and talked to him and his parents about the possible frostbite problems. Jarod took a deep breath. He remembered seeing on TV about two girls who had been stranded in a broken car in the middle of winter. One of them had had bad frostbite, and she'd lost her foot. He was scared to death that the same thing might happen to him. Finally, he made himself ask, "Dr. Maulken, could I lose my foot?"

"I don't think we're talking about anything that serious, but I have given your parents the name of a good doctor in Phoenix, and I want him to continue to monitor it."

Finally, Jarod and Jennifer were discharged, and the Goldens left the hospital to begin the trip back to Phoenix. Jarod thought of the silly songs his parents and sister had sung in the car up to the ski resort and the way he had pouted about having to be with them instead of his friends. Now the car was silent. It was as if they all felt too much to say anything at all. They passed the hotel where they had come to stay only days ago. "It seems like a very long time ago that we first came up here," his mother said.

Finally, his father switched on the radio, and other than the

DJ's voice and music, the car was quiet all the way home. Jarod felt his eyes stinging with tears when he first caught sight of the red tile roof of his house. During the night in the snow cave, there had been a part of him that had been sure he'd never see this house again. Back in his room, Jarod limped around touching the things on his desk and his dresser, almost as if to convince himself that he was really there and he was really alive. His left foot pained him every day, and for the first week they were home, both Jarod and Jennifer awakened with terrible nightmares of freezing on the mountain.

For the rest of the vacation, Jennifer and Jarod were content to stay at home and do nothing. In some ways, life seemed so normal that it was almost hard for them to believe they'd been stranded in that freezing snow cave, but in others, it seemed that no matter how normal life got, it would never again be quite the same for either of them.

School started again in January. Kids surrounded Jarod. No one wanted to talk about Jeff and Rick's ski trip or the slopes they'd snowboarded. In fact, no one wanted to talk about anything else except what had happened to Jarod. Lots of the kids had cut the newspaper articles about him and his sister out of the paper, and a few even wanted his autograph because he was famous. But it was strange. Now that he was the center of attention, he didn't really want to talk about his adventure. In fact, when school was over, he did something he never did. He ran to catch up with Jennifer, who as a third grader had gotten out of school fifteen minutes earlier than the sixth graders. As they walked home together, Jarod said, "Kind of a weird day, huh?"

"Yeah," Jennifer said. "It was. Everyone wanted to hear all about what happened. They all thought it was so exciting, and you know how I love to tell people stories, but I didn't want to tell them that one."

"Yeah," Jarod nodded in agreement. Memories of that freezing night filled their minds, and they walked home in silence.

Finally, Jennifer sighed and tried to smile at her brother, "Well, you didn't want to be plain and dull, and at least you weren't that. You didn't want to be just another kid here."

Jarod looked at his sister and half grinned back at her. "True. The kids at Miller all know who I am now. But now we've got a reputation to keep for being exciting. So, did you hear about those brothers who went bungee cording off a cliff? Want to try that! It'd be really awesome!"

"Jarod!" Jennifer stopped, stomped her foot, and said, "How can you even think about something like that?"

Jarod laughed, "Gotcha! Actually, plain and dull sounds okay for a while."

The End

ABOUT THE AUTHOR

An award-winning writer and teacher, Terri Fields was named Arizona Teacher of the Year in 1986 and to the *USA Today* "All-USA Teacher Team" in 1999. Terri's first book with Rising Moon, *Danger in the Desert,* was among those selected for the "Phoenix Top Kids' 100 Books" in 1998, a children's choice award. It was also nominated as an outstanding middle-grade novel in Arizona, Minnesota, and Illinois. Terri has published fourteen books and lives in Phoenix with her husband, Richard. They have two children, Lori and Jeff.